# BIG BAD WOLF

## THE LYCANS, I

JENIKA SNOW

**BIG BAD WOLF (The Lycans, 1)**

By Jenika Snow

www.JenikaSnow.com

Jenika_Snow@Yahoo.com

Copyright © January 2021 by Jenika Snow

First E-book Publication: January 2021

Second Edition: 2022

Photo provided by: Adobe Stock

Cover Designer: Cormar Covers

Editor: Kayla Robichaux

Proof Editor: All Encompassing Books

## Mikalina

It was spur of the moment, maybe reckless, definitely a shock to everyone I knew when I decided to take a trip across the ocean to a foreign country and stay for an undetermined amount of time.

Renting out a cottage in a tiny European village whose residents barely spoke English was the perfect escape from overbearing parents, fake friends, and a future that seemed bleak. And helping out an elderly woman with her shopping to earn some extra cash seemed easy enough.

Mindless, hour-long walks through the thick woods that surrounded said village also sounded ideal. No Internet. No television. And just the bare basics to get me by.

Perfection. Stress-free. Exactly what I needed.

Or maybe I was wrong about it all.

I felt someone or something watching me from the darkened, dangerous woods.

I felt someone—some*thing*—stalking me.

I didn't know what or who it was, but I knew with certainty it wasn't human... and that it wanted me.

### Ren

I wasn't human, not completely.

A Lycan—a centuries-old wolf-like creature that was feared by all, stronger than anything on the planet, and who was only ever after one thing.

My mate.

For over three hundred years, I had one purpose in life. Find *her*, the one female born to be mine. My female who'd cause the Linking Instinct—that supernatural connection that told me she was mine and I hers—to finally take root and make me whole.

And for hundreds of years, I'd been alone, saving myself for my mate, never stopping the search.

Until I scented her, saw her, finally felt my heart beat and the blood rush through my veins with hope and anticipation.

*Mine.*

She didn't see me, but she sensed me. And she ran. She couldn't possibly know how much the chase turned me on.

I didn't know how I'd make her understand I could never let her go, that nothing and no one would stop me from making her mine.

Because once a Lycan found his mate... nothing in this world, nothing supernatural or human, could keep him from her.

**Mikalina**

"You're crazy."

"This is ridiculous."

"Are you going through some kind of crisis?"

I closed my eyes as my parents' words reverberated in my head. After a moment, I reopened them and stared out the little airplane window.

Apparently, quitting your shitty job to pack up and leave for an undetermined amount of time and flying across the ocean to first sightsee through another continent before settling in a tiny Eastern European village in the middle of nowhere was now what constituted someone being mentally unstable. At least in my parents' eyes.

*God, I hate the window seat,* I thought ideally, bitching at no one yet feeling like the idiot my mother called me right before I left for the airport.

But when you do a spur of the moment thing like—oh, I don't know—empty out your savings, quit your job, and fly across the world for a little adventure, beggars can't be choosers.

I rubbed my eyes, dropped my hands to my lap, and saw the flight attendant start to come by. After calling her over, I gave an awkward smile to the person in the center seat, since I had to lean toward them in order to be heard.

"Can I get some booze?" Lord, yeah, I actually said that, asked it that way. "I-I mean, can I get a Bloody Mary?"

The flight attendant smiled and nodded before leaving. After giving my center seat neighbor another forced smile, which got me an equally tight —and very annoyed—grimace in return, I focused out the window again.

Before long, the flight attendant was coming back with my Bloody Mary. I didn't even care for alcohol all that much, and didn't like tomato juice either, but hell, since I was in the mind frame recently of doing things out of character, I just went with it.

First stop was landing in London. I planned on sightseeing for a couple of days before taking the Eurostar to Paris and checking out the catacombs. After that, a few more stops—Germany, Hungary, Poland. Then I'd end my little "vacation" as I headed east and settled on a tiny Romanian village nestled in the Carpathian Mountains.

Sounded pretty cut and dry to me, and despite trying to act like this was the best idea in the world... I was terrified.

I didn't know the land. I didn't know the language. And taking this trip was like throwing pudding against a tree and hoping it stuck.

But I'd been at a point in my life where everything else seemed lost. It felt as though I was running around in a circle, taking four left turns and always ending up at the same spot.

If all else failed and this trip turned out to be the worst idea ever, at least I'd have experienced a little more in life.

And that couldn't be so wrong, right?

# TWO

### Ren

My beast roamed within me, a terrifying creature that could claw a vehicle in half, take down any living thing that stood in its way, and gave me immense power.

I was a Lycan, one of the many supernatural creatures that inhabited the earth, my very existence known only to some. It was better—easier—to stay hidden, to not let humans know what I was. The weaker species feared too much, discriminated all, and were dangerous not only to themselves, but to anything they didn't understand.

I stalked the thick Carpathian Montane Conifer

Forest, the wilderness my home more than the castle in which I resided in my human form.

I built the castle centuries ago when I branched off from my family, started my own life, and started the lifelong search for my mate when I hit my adult years. To humans, I was nothing but a mere man—wealthy, isolated, reclusive... dangerous. That's what villagers would say when they heard my name.

Ren Lupineov.

It was safer to let them think I was dangerous, that my arrogance afforded me an air of authority and aristocracy. Let them believe my wealth was passed down from ancestors. For if they ever found out I was a three-hundred-year-old Lycan shifter—able to shift into a horse-sized wolf—they'd hunt me down with torches and axes.

They wouldn't succeed, of course. I could level anyone and anything that threatened me or mine.

*Mine.*

That lone word meant more than anything else... and not something I had for myself. And for the last three centuries, I'd been searching for my mate, hoping against all odds that my Lycan instincts would lead my Linked Mate—the one female who was born to be mine—to me.

I didn't know her name. Didn't know what she

looked like, sounded like, or if she was even on this continent. But I searched these woods every night, went from village to village, town to city, hoping my Lycan Instinct would somehow scent my mate, that I'd smell her and feel that *Link* between a Lycan and his mate, that supernatural connection that only a shifter had with his female, tying us together forever.

I didn't know if she was human, Lycan, vampire, or some other supernatural creature. I didn't even know if she was born yet, or had passed.

I stilled and brought a hand to my beating heart, rubbing my chest as a sudden onset of pain slammed into me at the thought I'd lost her before I even found her.

No, I didn't let those thoughts consume me. I wouldn't. I'd forever search for her. I'd forever stay positive that she was out there and I'd find her.

I stayed in my human form as I stalked the forest, my inner Lycan moving within me. The wolf tattoo that covered my entire back shifted along my skin, moved as the beast paced underneath. I didn't shift very often anymore, didn't allow the feral creature I housed to run wild. He was hard enough to control within me while I was a human, let alone when he had free reign of his surroundings.

And because he was snapping and snarling for our mate, it made him even more dangerous, destroying anything in his path. He was known to take our hundred-year-old oaks that stood in his way.

I curled my claws inward, the sharp points stabbing into my palms, drawing blood. Even though I was in my human form, I was still fearsome at a towering six-foot eight height, and three hundred pounds of solid muscle. But in my shifted Lycan form?

Nothing could match my strength and brutality.

My animal was front and center, moving right under the surface and showing itself. I knew my amber-colored eyes while I was a human changed to a glowing blue as he made himself known, trying to dominate.

*Not today, you impatient bastard.*

But still, the motherfucker pushed forward.

Fingernails as claws.

My body starting to become even taller, muscles becoming more pronounced with the need to shift.

Night vision perfect.

Canines unsheathing and descending.

Hearing and smelling even more accurate than any night predator.

I was the predator to predators.

I made my way closer to the village, finding myself drawn to the little Romanian town tonight for some reason.

The trees started to thin the closer I got, before opening up and showing Dobravina. I stood there and watched the villagers converse, shop, none of them having this eternal hole in their very being because they were missing the most important thing in the world to them.

Their other half. Their mate. The one person born to be theirs and theirs alone.

It made me jealous and angry, bitter and resentful. Humans may be one of the weakest species in the grand scheme of things, and I may be superior in strength, intelligence, and being a cunning hunter, but they had the only thing I wanted—love.

I wanted the love of my Linked Mate.

I tipped my head back and looked through the break in the trees at the sky. The full moon was coming, and it was coming fast. And when it did, I'd have no control over myself. Only my mate could ever calm me, could ever control the beast within me. It was her and her alone that held that power.

And for every full moon, the creature inside of me ripped and snarled, clawed its way out. And once it passed, once I was back in my human form and saw the destruction my Lycan wrought, that hole in my soul magnified all over again, and I yearned for my female even more.

I glanced at the village again, narrowing my eyes and getting even more pissed.

My Lycan snapped and growled, causing my human jealousy to grow tenfold as his rose as well. The tattoo on my back shifted and moved across the flesh, rising up slightly. I knew to the naked eye it would seem three dimensional. But my Lycan was pissed, as if he was telling me this was bullshit.

It was. *It so fucking is.*

# THREE

**Mikalina**

*Two weeks later*

I felt like I'd lived a thousand lives in the last fourteen days. It was crazy and wild, unexpected and such a learning experience that for the hundredth time since deciding to take this trip, I didn't regret it for one minute.

With my sightseeing behind me, I was finally in Romania, having taken a small aircraft to the tiniest airport I'd ever seen. Now, I was crammed into the smallest car known to man and going down an uneven and bumpy road, excited about the prospect of what this new journey held for me.

I couldn't even describe the feeling that churned

in me as I was taken closer to the little Romanian town of Dobravina. I'd never been there before, would have never even known about its existence if I hadn't decided to do this trip. But as I looked at the map, I swore something pulled me toward it, telling me that was where I'd finally find my peace.

I reached out and braced my hand on the handle of the door to steady myself, and had one foot pressed down hard on the floorboard in an attempt to not roll around the interior of the tiny tin-can-sized car.

Over the last fourteen days, I'd done the whole sightseeing thing through Europe. Eating exotic foods. Saw strange new lands. My camera was full of those experiences, memories that I'd be able to keep forever, even when I went back to my dull life— whenever that may be. As it was, this trip was open-ended, something that probably wasn't realistic, given the fact that I only had a certain amount of money to my name, but a reality I was going to try to make work.

Because I needed it, not only for my health, but for my sanity as well.

The little cottage I'd managed to rent had been found through a rental company. After contacting the owner, they told me there was the option of staying long term, and that they could discuss it when I got there.

Maybe I should've been more afraid of this whole situation, where I may have lost my damned mind. But there was something inside me, this flicker of light, this moment of feeling alive—hope —that told me this might very well be the best thing to happen to me.

This very well could be the exact thing I needed to reboot what was dead inside me.

We only lived once, right?

We only had a certain amount of days, a certain number of hours. A preordained amount of memories before the light in us was extinguished and we moved on to the next thing.

Whatever that was.

And I supposed I was just living that to the extreme, to the fullest, to experience all I could in the short number of years I had in this world.

The road evened out, and I was able to relax against the worn leather seat, my muscles aching from tensing during this trip. The driver was an older man with white hair, an unequally white thick beard, and eyebrows that looked like they were trying to crawl off his face because they were so bushy. His hands were curled around the cracked steering wheel, the skin tanned and worn, wrinkled and showing he'd no doubt done hard labor throughout his life.

He only said but a few words to me, and I had to wonder if it was because he didn't speak much English or if he just wasn't sociable. Either way, that was fine with me. I'd never been much for socializing anyway.

I looked out the window and stared at the thick line of trees that were passing us by in a blur. The radio he had on played some type of folk music, the volume turned down low, so I couldn't make out the words. Not that I could understand anyway.

I didn't speak Romanian. Although I did brush up on a few key terms before my trip, wanting to be respectful, so I could say thank you, please, and ask where the bathroom was. Things like that, although I just shook my head and once again felt like a complete lunatic for what I was doing.

The rental host, Andrei, had arranged the car ride—thank God for that, 'cause I'd for sure be up shit creek—and I realized I was putting a lot of trust in a complete stranger, but when in Rome, and all that.

The driver started to say something, his words broken but clear enough I knew what he meant.

We'd be there shortly.

He pointed to the forest, but I couldn't understand most of what he said. But I feel like I got the gist of it, as if he were... warning me? Maybe he was talking about wolves? Bears? Other wild animals that lurked in the dark, deep in the woods? A shiver wracked through me.

But I didn't think too much about any of that. It wouldn't do me any good. Instead, I shifted into the center seat and stared out the front window. I had my hands braced on the seat on either side of me, this car so old that the lack of seatbelts should've been horrifying, but instead, it transported me back to another time when people said "fuck you" to safety regulations.

The little town of Dobravina, Romania, came into view, and I actually sucked in a breath at how gorgeous the village was. Definitely transported back in time.

Nestled between the thick jut of trees that sprouted from the ground, it seemed quaint but mystical. When I'd been searching for places to stay, I knew I wanted to be somewhere east in Europe. I didn't know why I felt that pull, but it had been there, incessant, and there was no swaying my decision.

Maybe it was my curiosity and fascination with folklore, vampires and werewolves, demons and all those mythical things. And although I knew they were just stories, the very idea of being at the heart of where some of those tales originated seemed wildly interesting to me.

And here I was. In Dobravina, Romania.

The roads seemed to be made of cobblestone, and what was so strange was I already felt so... at ease. It was weird and exhilarating, and for the first time since I decided to take this life-altering trip, I really felt like this was the very best idea.

The little car bumped along, and I braced one hand on the door and another on the roof so I didn't crash against the top of the vehicle. After a minute, the driver slowed to a snail's crawl, and I relaxed once more, looking at the little shops that lined either side of me, staring at the people walking up and down the sidewalks, bags in their hands, older women wearing what I assumed was traditional-style clothing for this area. The younger generation was in typical jeans and T-shirts, the kids laughing and shouting at each other as they chased one another.

It was only another five minutes before the car pulled up beside the tiny cottage-like house. And when I said cottage, I meant just that. This house could've been a prototype for some fairy tale set in the middle of an enchanted forest.

Although small and clearly aged, it looked quaint and comfortable. The pictures online hadn't done it justice. Off to the side, I could see a garden, the tiny homes all around it holding the same charm.

After I paid the driver and thanked him, although I probably butchered the hell out of my translation, I stood there with my backpack slung over my shoulder and my duffel in my hand. I looked around, not sure if I should call the number that had been listed for the rental, but before I could think about it too much, a young man and an elderly woman came out the front door from the home directly beside the one I rented.

The young man lifted his hand and waved as he helped who I presumed must be his grandmother toward me.

"Mikalina?"

"Yes, but just Mika is fine."

He inclined his head and smiled. "I'm Andrei." His accent was thick and richly Eastern European. "This is my grandmother Mininya, although everyone calls her Mini. She's the owner of the cottage and lives right next door. She doesn't speak English, so I handle all the details of the rental, and the postings on the internet. You and I were communicating online."

Despite his accent, his English was impeccable. I smiled and offered my hand. After we shook, he started speaking with his grandmother. Mini was speaking quickly in her native language, but her focus was eerily trained right on me the entire time. She eyed me with intelligent eyes, then said something in a tone that suggested whatever agreement she'd come to, that was that and nothing would sway her. She gestured toward the house.

"Shall we go inside and look around?" Andrei asked and smiled but didn't give me a chance to respond as he led us toward the small house.

Mini started going on again, and he responded in an exasperated tone but nodded as if he knew he lost whatever fight was going on with the older woman.

"Is she okay? With this?" I tacked on that last bit, feeling as if maybe she didn't approve of me.

He waved off my concern and shook his head. "She's rambling on about nonsense. She's very happy you're here, I assure you."

Once inside, I was shown around to the quaint,

intimately confined space. The living room and kitchen were all one room with traditional folk accents throughout, bright colors and designs that made me feel like I was transported back in time. The bedroom was to the back, the bed tiny with a white lace bedspread. Andrei told me his grandmother wanted me to specifically know she quilted it when she was but fifteen years old.

Before I could comment on the beauty of it, she was speaking quickly again and pointing to things in the home, which Andrei translated just as fast.

The bathroom was small, the tub and toilet looking ancient. But it had hot running water, so I couldn't complain.

Finally, they showed me the backyard, and I actually gasped at the beauty of it. The small garden I'd seen in the front yard was only the tip of the iceberg. The garden extended all the way to the rear, even coexisting into Mini's yard. There were fruit trees and an array of vegetables, and sprinkled through all of this were beautifully colored flowers. It was quite a scene.

We made our way back to the front, where Mini started speaking again, her tone hard and unyielding. It was clear she got what she wanted, set in her ways, and I couldn't fault her for that. I looked at

Andrei when she was finished, expectant on what he'd say as he translated her words.

He nodded and relayed in Romanian before turning to me once more. "My grandmother wants me to ask if you'd join us for dinner tonight." His accent was thick and his smile was friendly. "But don't feel obligated. Your trip has been long, and she'd understand if you decline."

Although looking at his grandmother told me she probably would take offense. I was tired, but I didn't want to start things off on the wrong foot, so to speak.

"Um," I murmured as I looked between them. "Sure." I returned the smile. I faced Mini and told her "thank you" in her native tongue. She gave me a hint of a smile, as if pleased I replied in her language. Although I was pretty sure I butchered it with my accent.

After they left, I made my way back inside the cottage, my bags by the front door where Andrei had set them when he led me inside. Then I just stood there and looked around. I had to call my mother and let her know I got here safely, our video chats happening every few days so she knew I was still alive. I'd have to see if there was a place in town, or in a larger town close by, that had Wi-Fi, since it was clear there was none in Dobravina.

Then I'd have to see how my finances were faring. I didn't know how long I planned on staying here, but as I stood in the cottage—or more accurately, when I entered the village—I felt strangely... at home.

Comfortable and at ease in a foreign land.

I really had lost my mind.

# FOUR

## Ren

I sat in the leather recliner before the fire, a glass of bourbon in my hand, my focus on the flames. Another night alone. Another night staring into these flames until I got so fucking drunk I stumbled to my room before passing out.

I brought the glass to my lips and took a long pull from the crystal at the same time I heard an echoing *boom* from the very bowels of the castle. I closed my eyes and felt a deep-rooted sorrow as I listened to another maddening roar pierce through the thick stone of the manor.

I opened my eyes and finished off the bourbon, curling my fingers tightly around the glass, knowing

I should leave him be, but I found myself rising and making my way toward my only living relative.

After going through several doors, taking many hallways and corridors, I descended into the depths of the castle. The scent of moisture and earth filled the air. I stopped at the wood-and-wrought-iron door that kept me from my brother.

Luca.

Another roar came through, shaking the very foundation. The pain in that sound so fierce it nearly took me to my knees. I placed a hand on the scarred and weathered wood, closing my eyes and willing my older brother to find ease, even though I knew that wouldn't happen. Not without his mate.

He'd gone insane... because he hadn't found his mate. It was that hollowness in the pit of his soul that slowly encompassed him until he was mostly all beast, hardly any human left in him.

"Luca, be at ease. You'll be okay." I whispered the lie gruffly, and although I knew he heard me, he said nothing. There was a stillness for only a moment, then the sound of his heavy panting, of his footsteps as he paced back and forth, came through the stone and wood.

Luca had locked himself down here so long ago it was all I'd known anymore. He refused to be near anyone, and I felt like it was because he thought he'd somehow infect me with his madness.

He preferred his solitude and his insanity—but more acutely... his pain. I knew he stayed away to punish himself further, feeling like he failed for not finding his mate—worrying she was forever gone already.

The servants brought him food, water, ale, and anything else he required. I constructed a bathroom, knowing that although he couldn't care less about any essential needs because his mind was gone with thoughts of being mate-less, I hoped he'd take solace and a small measure of pleasure in the simple comforts.

"Luca? Will you not speak with me?" Every night, I came down here to talk with him, just to connect with him, to let my only remaining family know he wasn't alone.

I too was without a mate, but it was possibly because I was stronger in mind, maybe because I was younger than Luca, or hell, maybe I was just lucky to not be riddled with that crippling insanity that took some of the supernatural.

"I'm sorry, brother," I whispered gruffly. "I know the pain you feel. I know you want your mate. I know you crave that connection. I know you want that peace. I'm sorry I can't give it to you, brother mine."

"Leave me," Luca said in a guttural, inhuman voice. His tone was low, animalistic. It was distorted, and I knew although he was still in his human form, he was changed... possibly forever.

I couldn't see him, but I could imagine his once starkly handsome face took on more of a Lycan appearance, his canines permanently distended, his nails claws. His body was bigger and stronger despite his mind and heart being forever weaker.

I heard him scrape those vicious claws across the stone of the walls that he voluntarily imprisoned himself in, no doubt gouging great chunks out of the centuries-old stone that surrounded us.

"Will you not come out? Drink with me? Eat a meal with me?" My forehead rested on the door, my eyes closed. Despite the pain I felt for my brother and my need to help ease him, my thoughts were forever on *her*.

My mate. The female I had never met, never even seen.

She would forever be my priority, the only solace to calm me. She would always be at the forefront of my mind, and once I found her—if I ever found her —my sole goal would be to please her.

"Leave, brother, before I drag you down to this hell with me."

I exhaled and moved back, seeing the tray of partly eaten food left from earlier today. At least he ate—albeit not enough. Not nearly enough. But that fact told me Luca wasn't wholly lost.

There was hope, even if it was small.

Now, I just hoped we both didn't go to the depths of darkness for good, because then there would be no one to pull us out.

# FIVE

## Mikalina

I arrived at Mini's house later that evening for dinner. Andrei had knocked on the door and escorted me over, the conversation he started during the short walk friendly.

I was thankful he was eating with us, simply because if not it would be one hell of a clusterfuck trying to communicate with Mini. Not that I wouldn't try, but I didn't want to frustrate her with the language barrier.

And as I sat on her flower-printed, ancient-looking couch, I felt her eyes stray to me repeatedly. I felt strange around the older woman—not in a bad way, but more like she could look into my eyes and know everything I was thinking.

I felt as if she knew a secret about me—a very important one—that I wasn't even aware of. Like she knew the outcome of my future.

It was unnerving, to say the least.

It was a strange feeling to be so open and bare in the figurative sense, despite not being able to communicate with someone personally.

Mini insisted I sit and wait for dinner after I offered my help. She looked so aghast at me helping her cook that I felt my eyes widen and saw Andrei smirk and shake his head.

"It's not personal," he said as he came to sit on the couch beside me. "It's her way. And they are set in stone."

I nodded, although I couldn't say I understood. I'd never known anyone like that. "My grandmother goes to a country club every weekend," I said with distaste. "She's about as loving as a snowball to your face."

Andrei started laughing. "Things are much different here than your home."

"You have no idea," I murmured and looked around. Mini's living room was small but cozy, with the colorful folk decorations that somehow made me feel comfortable and right at home. She had a small TV that sat atop a polished table, a large lace doily underneath. Andrei had turned it on, telling me his grandmother liked to listen to the shows even though she didn't look at the screen.

The current show was what I'd call a soap opera, although I wasn't sure if it was called the same thing here. The woman was dramatically crying, clutching the strand of pearls around her neck as she clearly begged for the very handsome man in front of her to stay. She'd reach out to him only to snatch her hand back and glare, then start up with the crying again.

Although I assumed she was distraught he was leaving, I couldn't understand what was being said, so for all I knew, she could be cursing him out for having a small dick and not satisfying her in bed.

Mini started shouting from the small kitchen, and Andrei rose. "Dinner is ready. I hope you brought your appetite. My grandmother doesn't get to cook like she used to, so she's made a feast."

I smiled and followed him into the dining area and felt my eyes widen at the spread on the table.

"Oh my," I said low, my stomach growling at the sight and smells. Everything looked incredible and delicious. "She had to be cooking all day," I added absently, embarrassed that it had come out of my mouth.

"Oh yes. She was very excited to prepare dinner."

Mini gestured to the dishes and started rattling them off, which Andrei would then translate.

*Sarmale*—cabbage rolls. *Mămăligă*—polenta. *Mici*—grilled minced meat rolls, or something to that effect, as Andrei wasn't sure of the exact English translation. *Cozonac*—sweet bread. *Papanași*, which looked like tiny donut holes with delicious cream and jam on top.

He went on to name five other dishes, more desserts, and I was so overwhelmed but incredibly hungry.

I was grateful, never having anyone—not even from my family—go to this kind of trouble. I thanked Mini many times, and her smile coupled with a chin lift right before she waved off my gratitude told me she was proud I was pleased.

We sat down and began to eat, and Mini started speaking, Andrei once again translating. She described each dish and a memory attached to it, and I found myself transfixed with the stories, wishing I had a fraction of the upbringing she had.

She and her family didn't have much in the way of materialistic things, but what they did have was love and coming together as a unit over cooking and eating.

And to me, that sounded like heaven.

It was a far cry from my stiff, somewhat distant upbringing, where my modern-day parents were strict to the point they were cold at times. There hadn't been wonderful dinners where we sat around the table and talked about our days. There weren't memories attached to the dishes cooked or recipes passed down from other family members.

And wasn't that just sad as hell?

We sat there and ate, an hour and a half passing yet it seemed like no time at all. Mini stood and started clearing off the table, and I tried to help. I went to pick up a plate, but Mini spoke fast, her tone very disapproving as she shooed me away. Andrei just shook his head and smirked, gesturing for us to head out into the living room.

"Set in her ways," he said as if that was the key to everything.

She came out with coffees for us, then shuffled back into the kitchen. I felt bad I couldn't be of more help, but it seemed as if it would be an offense to her, so I followed Andrei lead us to the couch where we sat down.

The conversation between Andrei and me was light, with him asking about my life in the States. I reciprocated by asking him about his life here in Romania. I was fascinated to learn how different things were, how much harder he had to work for the things that had come so easily for me. It was also very clear that the normal day occurrences and conveniences in my life... I clearly took for granted, because to Andrei, they seemed as though they were luxuries.

Mini came and joined us shortly after and stayed silent as she sipped her tea and listened to Andrei and me speak about easy, normal things. But then the silence descended upon us, and I could feel this weird thickness in the air. I knew Andrei felt it as well, because he shifted on the couch, seeming as if he was uncomfortable with whatever was being charged around us.

That's when Mini started speaking, but not in her normal quick pace like I was accustomed to in this short time, but slow and steady, her eyes staring right at me as she continued to speak.

The way Mini spoke had a shiver racing up my spine, had goose bumps raised along my arms and legs. And the whole time, she stared right at me, looked right in my eyes, as if she were pleading with me, as if what she said was imperative.

"What is she saying?" I asked Andrei without breaking my focus on Mini. The older woman gestured toward the front door, presumably to the thick forest right outside. I didn't know why or how I knew what she was referring to, why I felt so strongly about it, but it was as real as the air I inhaled deep into my lungs.

I heard—and felt—the rise and fall of Mini's voice as she spoke, the tone and pitch of her words telling me she was explaining a story, telling a tale.

I glanced at Andrei, and he listened to his grandmother with this raptness on his face, as if he was hearing it for the first time as well. I glanced back at Mini, her old, wise eyes still on mine. Finally, she stilled, stopped, and leaned back, finishing her tea as she clearly waited for Andrei to translate whatever she just said.

I glanced at him, waiting expectantly.

He ran a hand over his jaw and shook his head.

"What did she say?" I asked with impatience, not meaning to sound that way, but feeling like I was at the edge of my seat, waiting for the finale of a story.

"She tells a story she heard when she was younger, about one of the wolves in the woods that frightens the villagers."

Mini said something else, and for some reason, I knew she was saying, "Tell her all of it."

But for some strange reason, the hairs on the back of my neck stood on end when I heard Andrei say "wolf."

"She says the story is of wolves. But they are different. They are..." He spoke to her again, and she answered immediately, her voice even and clear. "Lycan. She says they are not wolves but Lycan. Part man, part wolf-like creature."

My heart started racing for some reason at that, and I found myself glancing out the window. How strange to have this very physical reaction from that alone.

"The Lycans are a species that have been around millennia, before man, and will still be here after humans are gone." Andrei started speaking to Mini, and I focused on them again. He exhaled. "I'm sorry. I'm not sure why she's insistent on me telling you this. It's not to frighten you. She says you must know what lurks in the woods, because you being here is no accident."

I swallowed and knitted my brows. "I don't understand. No accident?"

He shrugged as if he didn't understand either. "She says nothing is coincidence. Everything happens for a reason. We are born to fulfill something."

Mini started speaking again, and I watched her, so engrossed for some reason that I actually found myself leaning forward, hanging on to the words she spoke that I couldn't understand.

"She says as soon as she looked into your eyes, she knew you were here for a reason, that you are meant to fulfill your truth. She says it's in your eyes."

For some reason, I lifted my hand, stopping when I got to the corner of one of my eyes. I didn't understand what she meant but it was clear she was very passionate about it.

I could push this all off to an older woman from a faraway land telling me a story she heard as a child and had hung on to it her whole life. But then Mini lifted her hand and gestured to her own eyes then pointed to mine. She started speaking again, her tone now becoming a lighter, gentler cadence. When she gestured for Andrei to translate, I snapped my head in his direction, anxious to hear more.

"My grandmother said something about blue eyes being fate, ones so bright they were not a human shade, but like the Lycans."

It was true, my eyes were a strange shade of blue, almost teal in appearance. As far as I knew, no other person in my family had this shade or anything remotely close to it. I'd gotten compliments as a child, looks from men and women in wonder, and appreciated it as I'd gotten older. I'd have to say my eyes were probably my best attribute, seeing as I was plain in every single manner aside from that.

But to think something so outlandish as this, whatever this was—not even including the whole wolf, Lycan, whatever folklore—that I had some kind of preordained destiny here simply because of the color of my eyes? Outrageous.

I kept that to myself, though. It was very clear Mini believed what she said wholeheartedly, and I was in no position to correct anyone and tell them I was nobody special. I didn't have a great destiny in front of me. I was simply here because I needed to get away, because I felt some kind of lacking in my life... some kind of pull to explore and move on.

I realized I needed to get away, how I felt so at home when I decided I was going to Dobravina, how I felt it was exactly where I was supposed to be. And that feeling intensified when I landed in the country, and even more so once I got to the village.

I stayed for another half hour, the conversation being steered in a more neutral, "safer" direction by Andrei. But all I could think about was what Mini said.

After thanking her once again, I headed next door but stood outside and stared at the thick line of trees I could see just up in the distance. The moon was high, not quite full, but casting a silvery, glowing light across everything. Shadows snaked between the trees, and it was pitch-black deep within those woods, so dense I saw nothing but that inkiness.

My skin felt tight, hot. My heart beat a steady rhythm, and I actually found myself moving closer to the woods, some unforeseen event almost drawing me closer. But I shook my head to clear it and forced—yes, I had to force—myself to go inside the cottage.

I found myself in my room and leaned against the wall, my mind even more confused than ever.

I went through the motions of getting ready for

the night, my mind thick with the tale Mini delivered.

And then I lay in my bed, the lights off, the sound of the night right outside my window doing nothing to lull me.

I knew there wouldn't be a restful sleep for me. Not when it felt like I'd touched a livewire.

### CHAPTER SIX

### Ren

I t was the same. Every night. A routine that came as natural as breathing.

As I walked the forest, my big body glided almost soundlessly over the terrain—a supernatural gift for all species of the supernatural world. We were—and always would be—stealthy predators. Beasts to be feared in the *Otherworld.*

I shoved my hands into the pockets of my waist-length wool coat, the night air warm enough that I didn't need it, but it had become a routine, it seemed.

My dark boots took the same path I did every night, over fallen branches, snapping the occasional twig, because I didn't care who or what heard me. I wasn't dressed for hiking, not with my dark slacks or my white, pressed button-down shirt. I was more aptly dressed for a meeting in the city than I was walking my grounds.

My Lycan was content for the time being, as content as a centuries-old supernatural creature who was impatient and desperate for his mate could be, that was.

A breeze picked up, pushing the short strands of my hair over my forehead.

And that's when I froze. My body tightening, my Lycan rising up faster than it ever had in my entire existence.

The scent. That smell that was so glorious, so sweet, so instantly addicting that my body went tight, my cock punching out, hard, demanding, only ever getting this way with thoughts of my mate.

*Mine. Mine. Minemineminemineminemine.*

Oh God, it was her. My mate, her scent flowing through the breeze, surrounding me in the sweetest way.

I closed my eyes and inhaled. And kept inhaling, drawing it all into my lungs, needing it inside me.

*I need her. Only her.*

My Lycan pushed forward, the need to claim her

so strong, but the moon wasn't full yet—a require-
ment for him to have enough strength to overpower
me completely. I pushed him back and swung my
head in the direction of town. Dobravina. She was
there. So close. So fucking close to me.

Before I could stop myself, I let the creature in
me have a little of the upper hand. Just a little, a
fraction, enough that I was slightly bigger, harder,
more primal and aggressive.

I ran through the woods, my feet pounding on
the hard terrain as I went closer to Dobravina. I had
one goal... find her.

*Finally. She's here. I've found her.*

I was all instinct right now, any rational,
coherent—human—thought vanishing the closer I
got to town... to her. My mate.

And when the trees started to thin out, and I
could see the lights of Dobravina up ahead, my pace
quickened, the very animalistic side of me taking
control. I was just about to break through the trees
and stumble into town when I forced myself to stop,
slamming my hand into a thick trunk of a tree, my
claws digging into the bark. That was the only thing
that grounded me in that moment, helping me still,
stay immobile.

I swung my head back and forth. Left and right. I

tipped my chin up and inhaled deeply, closing my eyes, groaning, growling. I still smelled the sweet albeit faint scent of her. And then I located the direction of where she was.

My feet were moving before I realized it was happening, my big body lumbering toward her, staying within the tree line, within the shadows. I knew I was more animal right now despite still appearing human. My canines were fully distended, my body bigger, taller. Thicker. My claws replaced nails, my eyes no doubt glowing that iridescent, neon-blue of my Lycan.

And then something pulled me to a stop. I stilled, staring at the small cottage just ahead of me. There. She was there. Her scent, although faint, was strongest here.

*Go to her. See her. Touch her. Mark her. Make her ours.* My Lycan growled and snapped, repeating those words in my head over and over again. Demanding them.

And then I was moving toward that house, my heart racing, my fingers curling and unfurling, my claws scraping into my palms and slicing the flesh. I stood just feet from the front door, staring at that closed wood that I could splinter as easily as if it were a toothpick, a fragile branch off a tree.

But then my instinct was pulling me around to the side of the cottage, toward a small window in the back. The glass was cracked slightly at the corner, and a low, rumbling growl left me as I inhaled again, her scent so concentrated right then that I actually swayed.

My cock was thick and hard, my hips rolling on their own. I needed her desperately. I needed to mark her, claim her. I needed to spread her thighs, hold her in place as I feasted between her legs, as I sucked at that sweet honey that would no doubt spill from her. For me. Only me.

Sweet Jesus, I was losing my mind with need.

I moved closer to the window and peered inside, the light from the moon and the open curtains allowing me to see her clearly, my night vision acute and crystal in clarity.

Gods... there she was. The ground shook, rumbled again beneath me. No one would ever be able to feel it but me, the very world shaking because I found *her*.

She slept on a small bed across from where I stood, her dark hair fanned over the stark-white pillow. The blanket was pulled up to her chest, the perfect swells of her breasts rising and falling evenly as she slept.

But then her brows furrowed low, her body starting to shift under the sheet. She sensed me, knew I was near. But her fragile mind couldn't understand why she felt this way.

Who was she? Where did she come from? She wasn't from the village. I knew that just from looking at her, just scenting her. I would've known she was here if she lived in Dobravina.

No, she was new, probably having just arrived. I'd have sensed before now if the case were any different.

I had my hands on either side of the cottage, my claws digging into the stone. It crumbled easily under the onslaught. I was doing everything in my power not to crash through that window and throw her over my shoulder, take her back to my castle... back to her home.

*Our* home.

And then her eyes opened and she glanced at me, the sharp intake of breath coming from her. I groaned anew, rolled my hips again and again, my body swaying back and forth from the intensity of my need for her.

Her eyes. So blue they glowed. The color of mine... of my Lycan's. I knew she was still deep in sleep, her focus unseeing, her body knowing what I was and being inexplicably drawn to me.

"Sleep, *iubirea mea.*"

Her eyes closed easily on the command, as if she'd heard me, as if I whispered those words intimately against her ear.

I wanted to desperately go to her. I'd waited three hundred years for this female, and here she was, just feet from me, only that fragile rock and glass keeping me from the one who was meant to be mine.

But I'd only frighten her, the intensity in which I needed her so strong she'd be terrified. And that was the last thing I wanted to do. My sole goal, the only thing my instinct demanded of me, was that I protect her. *Make her happy. Keep her safe.* Above all else, I needed to make her happy and give her anything she wanted.

So I could wait. I had to. Just for a short time. I'd learn about her and pray that she came to me of her own free will before the full moon. And it was quickly approaching.

Because once it was full and high in the sky, my beast would take over, the need to mate and mark her so strong there would be no denying it.

Gods. She was here. I'd finally found her.

# SEVEN

**Mikalina**

I had the strangest dream, although I couldn't remember the details. But it stuck with me all morning. And no matter how hard I tried to recall it, it was fleeting like mist.

I scrubbed a hand over my eyes as I sat at the table, my breakfast of fruit and tea mainly unconsumed. I pushed the plate of fruit away and stood, walking out the front door because I was too anxious to sit still. I saw Mini working in the garden and lifted my hand in a wave, although she wasn't even looking at me, too focused on her work.

From last night, I knew Andrei lived out of town in one of the larger cities. He worked as a computer analyst—whatever that entailed—and came once a week to see Mini. Although he'd given me his number in case I needed a translator or anything else, I knew I had to figure out what I was going to do.

*What am I going to do now?*

My mind was calculating how much money I still had saved versus when I expected to go home. I cringed internally. Going home. Why did that feel so... wrong?

I didn't know what kind of job opportunities I could possibly have here, what with not speaking the language, not even being a citizen, and not having a vehicle.

God, was this all one huge mistake, even if it felt like the very best thing in the world?

I found myself walking toward the woods, but something had me looking over my shoulder. Mini was standing and staring at me, and then surprising the hell out of me as she lifted her hand and shooed me along. Was she telling me to keep going? Was she telling me to move away? I didn't know, but my feet must have, because I kept walking forward.

There was a small footpath at the edge of the tree line, and I made my way along it, the sun streaming through the leaves, the sound of birds overhead almost a lullaby.

I didn't know how long I walked, but the sun felt good through the breaks in the trees, the breeze felt nice on my skin, and the sounds and smells around me had me closing my eyes and just... feeling.

I felt this lightness, but then that easiness kind of dissipated as something tighter, harder, stronger settled within me. I slowed and then stopped, looking around, unsure what I was feeling, but knowing it was... intense.

Seconds passed. Maybe minutes. And then it hit me.

This feeling. The intensity. The thickness all around me.

*Someone's watching me.*

*I'm not alone.*

My heart started to pound harder as I looked to my right. My left. In front of me. Behind me.

I spun around. Around and around. The hairs on the back of my neck stood on end. On my arms.

I panted.

*God, someone's watching me.*

The flight instinct was running rampant inside me, so I turned and started heading back toward the village, telling myself not to run. And with every step I took, I continued to tell myself that maybe this weird feeling was just in my head.

I'd been thinking a lot about Mini's story from last night, picturing what these Lycans looked like, what their fire felt like under my skin—you know, things a crazy person would ponder.

Would I fear one if I saw it in person? Would I run from it?

I shook my head at the ridiculous thought. See one? As if they were real.

And then there was my dream, the one I couldn't remember but felt like was right there at the surface of my consciousness. It was a strange and confusing feeling, and as I slowed to a more reasonable pace, I tried to reason with myself that's all this was.

An overactive imagination—my body making something in my mind physical.

I forced myself to stop and look around, telling myself over and over again that it was nothing. There was nothing there, no one watching me. I gave a nervous laugh, but still I walked toward the village. I ran my hands up and down my arms, trying to push the chill away even though it wasn't cold out.

But the strangest thing out of all of this was... I wasn't afraid.

I felt like someone watched me, that there was something out there I couldn't see, yet I felt no fear. I just felt... awareness.

I stepped through the tree line and headed right toward the front door of the cottage. I'd call my mother. I shook my head and snorted internally at that thought. I must've really been freaked out if I was resorting to making an expensive, overseas call to my mother.

Before I went into the house, I stopped and looked over my shoulder, scanning the tree line once more. I saw nothing, but I still felt as if I wasn't alone. A shiver moved along my arms, and I forced myself to go inside. I closed the door and leaned against it, shutting my eyes and telling myself it was all in my head.

*All. In. My head.*

Yet why did it feel so real and make me feel... alive?

# EIGHT

### Ren

I'd stay in the woods all night, watching that cottage, waiting for my mate to emerge. I had to see her, wanted to hear her voice, get a concentrated inhale of her sweet scent.

The instinct to go to her was fierce in me, a war drum that beat fast and hard, demanding I make her mine.

The minutes turned into hours, and soon the moon was falling away as the sun rose. But I'd wait out here all day for her, wait my entire fucking life if that's what it took for me to get another glimpse of my female.

I wanted to watch as the wind blew through the

strands of her dark hair, teasing the ends so they moved along her shoulders.

I wanted to see every detail that made up her facial features. I wanted to stare into her Lycan-like eyes and pull her in close, push the hair off her shoulder, and strike her neck to mark her.

And then she finally emerged, and all rational, conscious thoughts left me.

And she was even lovelier in the morning sun.

*Absolutely gorgeous.*

*Perfection.*

*Mine.*

Never could I have pictured my mate to be so ethereal, so perfect for me in every way. It was as if she'd been plucked out of every fantasy I could have ever conjured. Made just for me. Only for me.

She was so small compared to me, half my height, her body lithe yet curvy. She seemed fragile, delicate.

*Tiny.*

I had to curl my claws into the trunk of the tree once more, forcing myself to stay hidden, to not go to her and take her to the ground to claim her like the animal I was. Christ, I wanted to sink my canines into her pretty neck good and hard so every Lycan would know she was mine.

I wanted them to gaze at the slender column of her throat and see how fiercely I marked her, laid claim to her.

But I didn't go to her. I just watched.

She walked the trail of the woods, her brows pulled low as if in deep concentration. I wondered what she thought about. I wondered if her subconscious remembered me from last night, maybe feeling as though she had an intense dream but unable to pull up the details.

And then she sensed me. I heard the way her heart started beating faster. I could smell the perspiration start to line her perfect flesh. All those reactions were so strong it was as if they were happening to me, our *Link* so intense there was no denying what she was to me. What I was to her.

I could've stayed right in the entrance of the forest—staring at where she resided, hoping to see her again—all fucking day. And I would have if I didn't have to go back to the manor and check on Luca. I had to make sure he was well.

*I have to tell him about my mate.*

I wanted to tell my brother that I found her. I wanted to let him know there was hope, that he was next. I wanted my brother to know that after all these long centuries, his mate was, in fact, out there. Waiting for him.

I hoped he felt relief, maybe a semblance of calmness that he couldn't give up... that he shouldn't.

I focused on my female once more, my entire life revolving around her now.

I knew what my mate looked like. Knew her scent. It was now forever ingrained in me, both of us linked in that inescapable, undeniable, and unbreakable way. There was no place in the world she could go that I wouldn't find her. There was no place she could run that I wouldn't give chase. And I knew I wouldn't be able to hold back from claiming her much longer.

I just hoped before the full moon rose she would be ready to give herself to me completely.

Because I didn't think I could control myself where she was concerned.

CHAPTER

# NINE

**Mikalina**

I stayed inside the rest of the day, not because I was afraid, but because I felt... off. Different even.

It was so strange to explain or even try to describe to someone. I was still me, still felt like I was the same person, but it was almost as if a switch had been turned on, one I had no idea about, didn't even know existed.

I swore everything was crisper, clearer. The smells of the flowers in the garden, the scent of my tea, the warmth from the steam rising up from the mug.

I swore I could hear the kids playing outside as if

I stood right beside them. I didn't know what was wrong with me, maybe just my nerves, a very overactive imagination.

I tried to busy myself by calling my mother. She hadn't answered, and a part of me had been relieved. That couldn't be normal or even healthy—to not want to converse with your parents, knowing there really was no connection there, no solid foundation.

Weariness settled in my bones, and I rubbed my eyes, feeling tired all of a sudden.

For the last hour, I'd been looking over my finances, seeing how much I had saved versus how long I could realistically stay here.

Enough, but not for me to make this my home.

I didn't want to be broke by the time I went back to the States, and at that moment when I thought about actually going home—or what I'd always considered home but maybe never felt like that—left a sour taste in my mouth, a knot in the pit of my stomach.

Home was where your heart was... or something like that.

I could've told myself that I was looking over my finances and all of that because I needed to just go, to understand I could still be independent when I went back to America. But the truth was deep down I knew I was looking over everything, because I *didn't* want to go.

"I'm losing my damn mind," I said to no one, alone in this little kitchen, feeling isolated, although I really wasn't.

### chapter TEN

Luca

I listened to my brother's retreating footsteps and took note he moved slow but steady.

He wanted me to call him back, to open my emotions as he just had.

To give him hope that I wasn't truly gone and mad.

I wasn't going to reassure him though. I couldn't.

He found his mate, and I was happy he would no longer suffer the same lonely fate we had all these centuries. But jealousy reared its ugly head at hearing he was now completely whole, even if he hadn't claimed her yet.

He found his mate, and that's all that mattered.

I felt fucking sick and angry at myself for feeling anything but joy and happiness for him.

I knew Ren had told me in hopes of giving me a renewed sense of purpose. I knew that without a doubt. I felt it in the way he spoke, the inclination of his words. I refused to open the door for him, but even still, his muffled words had been as if he was standing right before me, baring his soul.

I sat on the edge of the bare mattress that sat flush with the cold, stone floor, my knees bent, my feet planted firmly on the unforgiving rock.

Dragging a hand through my hair, my mind whirled with the pain, discord, and loneliness that some of the supernatural succumbed to when they didn't have their other halves. Their mates.

A mind slowly declining, wasting away as thoughts and images of that unnamed soul that was meant for you and you alone.

Lycans with their Linked Mates.

Vampires with their Coveted Ones.

Demons with their Blood Females.

And an array of other supernatural creatures I heard lost their fucking minds because they hadn't been mated.

We were strong beings... the strongest to walk

the earth. Yet in this regard—to that one female—we were utterly weak.

Reality twisted as I sat in this... hole at the pit of the castle. My home forevermore. A place to stay away from others so I didn't inflict my sickness on them. This may not be a virus one could catch, but it sure as hell felt like one, spreading outward, a parasite to claim a host.

Leaving was an option, allowing my brother to be with his female in our ancestral home, away from the darkened likes of me.

Ending my suffering was also an option, although my belly clenched and churned at that thought.

For even through my hopelessness, a sliver of possibility that *she* was still out there—my beautiful, perfect mate—waiting for me, had me hanging on.

For what if I left this world, taking matters into my own hands, but she still walked the earth? I couldn't leave her if the possibility was still there.

Screams erupted in my head, and I squeezed my eyes shut, roaring out, the pain unimaginable. My mind slowly slipped away day by day until I was more beast than man.

I roared again, swiped at the mattress, stuffing

and feathers exploding upward from my violence. I destroyed the room, the anger in me—my beast rising up—so monumental it consumed me.

And this was all because I didn't have the one meant to be mine.

It was easier to lose your mind than think there really was no hope.

# ELEVEN

**Mikalina**

I'd gotten the call from Andrei just an hour before, Mini knocking on my front door and gesturing for me to follow her. There, she pointed to a yellow, ancient-looking corded phone attached to the wall, the receiver hanging against the wall, the coiled cord stretched taut.

Andrei hadn't been able to make it out of the city to see Mini and do her weekly shopping, so he asked me if I'd mind. He'd been so apologetic, as if asking had put this massive burden on me.

I assured him it wasn't, that I was actually glad to have a task to do. Although I didn't tell him it was to keep my mind off everything else.

It had only been twenty-four hours since the forest incident—which hadn't really been an incident at all, to be honest. Me freaking out over absolutely nothing didn't make a scene out of some horror movie.

So here I was, a few bills of cash Mini had given me tucked into my wallet, and a shopping list as long as my arm in my pocket. Andrei told me the large grocery shop was in the next town over—which he said the footpath was the fastest route, even if I'd taken a car. Which I didn't have, so this was my only option.

Back in the forest I went.

And as I stood by the entrance, hearing the birds overhead, feeling the breeze along my skin, smelling the wilderness and all the glorious scents of nature, I felt this strange eagerness consume me.

Taking a deep breath, then exhaling slowly, I just told myself to act like the adult I was and push whatever weird feelings I'd been having away.

The next town over was a good twenty-minute walk through the woods. The sun was high in the sky, and even with the thick canopy of trees overhead blocking out a lot of the light, there was enough illumination and breaks in the branches that there were no darkened corners to add to my already growing uneasiness.

I took the trail, keeping a steady pace, and the longer I went, the deeper I walked, the more I felt... at ease.

I occupied my mind by thinking about what I needed to get for Mini. Although the shopping list was in Romanian, Andrei told me all I had to do was give it to the grocery store clerk and they'd know what to do.

I tried to think about anything and everything, just enjoying the walk, but I felt that tickling on the back of my neck, that almost sixth sense, an awareness of everything around me.

A twig snapped in the distance, and I didn't let myself get tense about it.

A flock of birds took flight above me, shadows cast along the ground by their wingspans moving through the broken patches of the canopy. I wouldn't even contemplate if something frightened them. That's why birds scattered that way, right? A threat. A predator.

But the longer I walked, the more the seconds turned into minutes.

More twigs snapped behind me, to the left, then to the right. I moved away from them as I heard the noise, this feeling directing me to go this way, that way, keep focused and walking.

And after a while—time seeming to go so fast yet slow down all at the same time—I looked, realizing I had no idea where I was, that I wasn't on the path any longer.

The trail underneath me started to become less worn, as if it wasn't taken regularly. I stopped and glanced around, trying to decipher where I was.

*Stay on the trail*, a voice in my head spoke loudly, and I found myself moving again, staying on the trail that clearly wasn't worn, hoping it would open up and I'd find myself back in the village, or to my original destination in the next town over.

But the more I walked, the deeper I realized I was going into the forest, where the trees became thicker, the sunlight starting to not pierce through the branches as much. Once again, that flight or fight instinct grew in me fast and hard. My palms started to sweat, my hands shaking slightly. My movements weren't as sure, and I stumbled over twigs and rocks that I otherwise would have clearly missed.

I didn't know how long I'd been walking, well over half an hour, plenty of time for me to have reached town. But I was still stuck within the woods, the hardly taken trail still underneath me the only thing making that panic stay below the surface.

Clearly, this led somewhere. But where?

I walked for another five minutes and noticed the thinning of the trees. And then I saw something in the distance. I walked faster, my feet taking me over the terrain effortlessly now.

And as the trees thinned out and the massive stone structure came into view, I actually stumbled, reaching out and placing my hand on a tree trunk.

One thing came to mind.

*That's a fucking castle.*

I was mesmerized by the sheer size of it, the detailing, the stonework... everything.

I found myself moving toward it before I could stop myself or before I even realized what I was doing.

# TWELVE

### Ren

I hadn't wanted to frighten her... but I meant to steer her in the direction of my estate. I ushered her unknowingly left, then right, up a hill, down toward a ravine, then straightened her direction.

I kept her straight after that, leading her closer to my ancestral home—*her* home by birthright as being my mate.

I needed to accelerate the process of her knowing me, needing me, feeling that Linked connection the Lycan male felt with his female.

I stared up at the morning sky as if I could already see the full moon. I closed my eyes as though I could feel the silvery glow on my flesh, as if I felt the power that came with it as it seeped into the Lycan side of me.

The full moon was coming and it was coming fast.

I moved quietly and slowly toward her, so fucking pleased she was here. Finally. Here. My blood was humming right under my flesh, my Lycan wanting to shift so he had this opportunity with our female.

No. I wouldn't give up this moment with her. He'd have the full moon.

She was up by the garden, the flowers having been planted by the staff just the night before. I wanted everything perfect, clean and prepared. I had them work around the clock in preparation— and in hope—that she wouldn't put up any resistance to what we'd have together.

*That she's mine.*

I might be overly optimistic, most definitely presumptuous, seeing as she was human and probably had no idea about my kind, but I didn't fucking care. I couldn't accept any less.

I was so focused on her, watching as she moved around the property, the way she looked at everything her big eyes could take in, that I didn't see the large twig underneath my foot. It snapped in half, the *crack* echoing all around, the trees making the sound travel everywhere.

She spun around, her gaze going right to me as I stepped into the clearing. Her eyes widened, and I heard the sharp intake of breath as she let those so familiar, so beautiful blue eyes travel over me.

She didn't know me, but in that moment, she was most definitely recognizing me.

**Mikalina**

# THIRTEEN

**Mikalina**

The man standing in front of me was no man at all. Well, he obviously was, but he wasn't any male I'd ever seen in my life. He seemed... more.

Even from the distance that parted us, I swore I could make out every detail of him. He was tall, unbelievably, ridiculously tall. God, he had to be six-foot seven, maybe even an inch or two more than that. He was most definitely a foot taller than my five-foot six stature.

His shoulders were wide—so wide I swore he blocked out the forest behind him.

And even though he was fully dressed—a point

that kind of had me feeling disappointment, seeing as I bet he looked incredible naked—it was very clear this man was ripped.

He was huge, in one word. Tall. Big. Muscular to the point I felt tiny. Double, maybe even triple my size.

And his face... good God... that face was rugged and handsome, with a square jaw, masculine hollows under his cheeks, a straight, perfect nose, and lips that were full and fit him perfectly. His hair was short and dark, the strands looking utterly soft, like silk, as they lay across his forehead.

He seemed too much male.

Too.

Much.

Everything.

Almost inhuman in his attractiveness, in the size of his body, the masculinity that poured from him.

My body reacted to his very presence instantly. Warming. Softening. Getting wet.

But despite all of those physical things I was currently shamelessly checking out, the one thing that struck me as monumental was the fact that I felt like I *knew* him.

He took another step, and although I should

have felt fear, I didn't feel anything but this strange calmness steal over me at his very presence.

"I'm sorry. I don't mean to trespass," I stammered out, feeling embarrassed that I'd been caught walking around someone's property.

The man said nothing but stopped, closed his eyes, and I swore his big body swayed as if he were relishing the sound of my voice. The distance between us was great enough that I couldn't quite make out every little detail of his face, but when he opened his eyes, I swore I saw his irises flash a brilliant blue before vanishing and being replaced by an amber color.

A blue that looked... exactly like my own eye color.

*No. Not possible. A trick of the light.*

"No need to apologize," he finally said, his accent thick, his voice richly deep and almost hypnotic.

I instantly felt myself relaxing at the sound. It was now my turn to sway, the sound of his voice so deep and masculine that I could grasp why it affected me the way it was.

He kept his focus trained on me as he came closer, sweeping a massive arm out and swinging it to the side as if to show the land. "What's mine is yours."

I felt my brows pull down low. *What an odd thing to say.* I reasoned the language barrier may have contributed to his weird choice of words.

"This is your property, your home?" I looked behind me at the massive stone structure once again, in awe of it. When I faced forward once more, a startled gasp left me at the fact that he stood right before me. God, he was big... huge. I had to look up and up... and up some more just to look into his face.

"This is my home," he rumbled out. His voice was smooth, yet I sensed sharp edges around it. The sound instantly had me warming.

"It's beautiful." The words were low, murmured in a very pleased manner. I instantly felt my face heat at the way I sounded.

"I agree. Very beautiful," he responded, yet he was looking at me, staring into my eyes as if he most definitely was not speaking about his home.

I didn't understand my very physical reaction to him, let alone his voice, but I didn't care too much to try and fight it.

Because it made me feel good.

"Ren Lupineov," he introduced himself, holding out his big hand for me to take.

I lifted mine and slipped it into his, his palm three times the size of mine as he engulfed my hand, his flesh warm, smooth, sending electricity slamming up my forearm and right to the center of my chest. I actually gasped from the contact and how instant it was.

This low rumble surrounded me, and I realized it came from Ren. He was... growling.

I couldn't move, let alone breathe as I stared into his eyes, and once again I swore I saw them flash blue before turning a warm amber color again. I slipped my hand from his, and for a moment, I felt his resistance in letting me go, but he did, and I didn't miss how he curled his fingers inward as if to stop himself from reaching out again. I had no damn clue why I knew that, but I felt that truth in every part of me.

"Mikalina Poppet." My voice was low, breathy, and I should have been embarrassed by the latter, but I didn't care enough to divert my feelings to anything else but this warmth Ren sent up and down my spine.

"Mikalina."

*Oh God.* The way he said my name made this needy sound leave me, and humiliation immediately rose up inside me. I snapped my eyes open, not even realizing I closed them as he'd all but purred out the name I heard my entire life but had never reacted to hearing it like this before.

"Would you like a tour?" At my hesitation, he added, "Of the grounds?"

I was a little frozen in that moment, my mind totally heightened yet relaxing because he was asking something as mundane as giving me a tour of his place. But was it really mundane? The way he asked it, the inclination of his voice, led me to believe my answer was pretty damn important. And I realized... he was holding his breath as he waited for me to respond.

I licked my lips and knew I should feel some semblance of uneasiness, *right*? I mean, I didn't know this man, and I really shouldn't be contemplating letting him show me around. For all I knew, he had prisoners chained up medieval style in the depths of his massive home.

*Get a grip.*

"I don't have a lot of time. I'm supposed to be heading to the market for some things but got turned around, which is how I stumbled upon your home." I looked around, knowing I was rambling, but I was really damn nervous. "And I need to get there and return to Dobravina before it gets dark."

He said nothing, just smiled in a sexy aristocratic way and held his arm out for me to take, as if he came from another time.

And what do you know... I found myself slipping my arm through his as if it was the most natural thing in the whole world, like I hadn't just made a shitload of excuses on why I couldn't walk around his property with him.

Just like that, I let this sexy-as-sin male—not just a man, but very much *male*—walk me around his property, knowing there had to be something wrong with me to want this so. Damn. Much.

# FOURTEEN

**Ren**

I'd shown her the exterior of the property and wanted to show her the inside, but in due time, I told myself. Little steps to get her used to me, to my presence. Things would move quickly once she was mine, and I wanted her to come to terms with all of this in her own way.

"Thank you for showing me around. It's all so gorgeous." She glanced over her shoulder at the estate again, this wistful expression on her face. "I do have to go though. Someone is waiting for me to bring back supplies they need."

"Please," I gestured for her to go ahead of me

"Let me take you there. It's just a short walk through my property to the next town over, and I can't in good conscience let you travel the woods alone."

*Because I have to be with you. I can't leave you. It physically pains me.*

She gave me the prettiest smile, and just as she nodded and was about to step onto the trail, the deep, rumbling roar of my brother gone mad sliced through the stone, as if shaking the very stone of the manor.

Mikalina whipped around to stare at the estate, her eyes wide, the scent of her fear coming through sharply.

"It's nothing," I said low, my Lycan rising up at the scent of her fear. My inner animal wanted to protect her, even though I knew what the "threat" was. "Wild animals litter the forest surrounding the estate. They won't dare come close." *Because one is already inside the manor. One is deep inside* me. "After you, sweetling."

She didn't comment on the endearment, probably still too shocked by what she'd heard.

But the farther we walked from the manor, the more her fear abated, and her curiosity of her surroundings—and me—intensified.

I couldn't keep my eyes off her. The way the sun streamed through the branches and hit her dark-brown hair, showing me the golden-red highlights. The way the breeze picked up every once in a while, teasing those strands, and sent the most luscious scent up to my nose had every part of my body tightening.

I was drawn to her, her body every single thing I could've ever wanted. It was like she was plucked for my very fantasies, no part of her undesirable to me. I meant it when I said she was perfect.

"Your house is gorgeous," she said again, and I liked that she kept mentioning it. It made me proud and had my chest puffing up at the fact that my mate was pleased with *our* home.

And it was ours.

She might not know it yet, but she would. Very soon.

"It's been in my family for generations." I left out the part that I'd been the one to build it centuries ago... in preparation for when I finally found her. I was pretty sure that little bit of information would probably shock the hell out of her.

We were silent for a few more steps, but I could've stayed like this forever.

Both of us quiet.

Both of us speaking.

Or hell, just listening to her talk was enough for me to be happy. It didn't matter what we were doing as long as she was with me.

And her voice... gods, her voice was calming, soothing.

"Do you have family here? Do they live with you?"

My chest swelled with pleasure that my female wanted to learn about me. I cleared my throat and glanced away, wanting to tell her everything. I wanted her to know about me and my life, that for the last three centuries she'd been the only focus of mine. I wanted my mate to know everything I had was here, that I created my life with the sole reason to please her.

"It's just my older brother and me now. He lives with me." Slowly losing his mind in the pits of the manor. "Our parents passed some time ago." My mother died in a tragic accident, and my father couldn't live without his mate. He passed just a week after of a broken heart.

"How much older is your brother?"

*He's nearly four centuries old, sweetling.* "He's a

good bit older than I am." We walked for a while more, the silence not uncomfortable, but I wanted to hear more of her voice. It calmed me in more ways than I could ever describe. "My brother isn't... well." I didn't know why I told her that; maybe because I wanted her to know all there was about me.

She stopped and looked at me, her eyes conveying her sympathy. "I'm sorry your brother is sick."

Although I didn't want to talk about Luca, and didn't want to bring a shadow of darkness to this moment I had with Mikalina, connecting with her on this level had me feeling even closer with her. But I would never keep anything from her, never lie. So, I exhaled slowly and thought about how I would broach the subject. I couldn't very well tell her the whole truth at the moment, about why Luca lost his mind, but she would know in due time.

"He lost someone," I responded. "The most important person to him." It wasn't a lie, but not the whole truth. He had lost someone... his mate, in retrospect to him, because he hadn't found her yet. "And he's not handling it well, as can be expected."

She looked at me then, and her blue eyes could have brought me down to my knees for the empathy that shone in them. "I'm really sorry to hear that."

She held my focus for a moment and then looked forward again, her throat working as she swallowed, her expression and the tone of her voice so damn genuine and sincere that I wanted to pull her in and kiss her until this darkness was gone.

The fact that she showed sympathy toward my brother—a total stranger to her—made me fall in love with her instantly.

"I've never experienced that kind of loss—the kind that sucks the very life out of you, but I can imagine it's very crippling." Her voice was so low, so meaningful.

She had no idea how debilitating it truly was to lose hope that you'd never find your mate.

"I hope he finds peace soon."

And once again, I wanted to pull her in close and just hold her, whisper words of endearment in my native tongue against the shell of her ear. I wanted to thank whoever was listening that I had this extraordinary female as my mate.

And I nearly did reach out for her and do just that, but then she lost her footing and started to fall over from a large root that erupted from the ground. I had her in my arms just seconds later, her body pressed to mine, every part of me humming and singing in pleasure at how good this felt.

She stared up at me with wide eyes, her shock one of adrenaline that she'd almost fallen, or maybe it was because I'd caught her so swiftly and still held her close.

Maybe it was a little bit of both.

"Thank you... for that. For not letting me fall on my face."

*I'll always catch you. I was born to be strong so I could protect and provide for you.*

She pulled away far too soon—to my disappointment—and the sheepish look she gave me told me she was embarrassed that she'd clung to me. And she most definitely had, her little hands gripping my shirt as if she were afraid to fall once more.

Did she realize she clung to me? Pulled me closer?

She cleared her throat and started walking again but stayed silent. I didn't press for conversation, just enjoyed being in her presence, having her scent surrounding me, slipping into my body. I'd never felt so complete in my life, and I hadn't even claimed her yet. I could only imagine the monumental change within me once I finally had her and was buried deep between her sweet thighs, my fangs gripping her shoulder as I gave her my mark.

All too soon, we were entering the town of

*Lankalinov.* But I had no intentions of letting her be alone. Listening to her talk, feeling complete for the first time in my life, had me greedy for more time with her. So I gestured for her to go before me and let my gaze linger on the perfect roundness of her ass. My heart thundered, my cock punched forward, and I tried to discreetly adjust myself so she couldn't see my raging hard-on pressing against my slacks.

Mikalina stopped and glanced over her shoulder at me, clearly surprised I followed behind. "You're coming with me?"

I gave her a smile, one I hoped conveyed that I was being polite, when in reality I didn't want her to be alone, didn't want any males to look upon her. Although that might be a dangerous combination, because if I were to see someone gazing at her, my inner animal would snarl and growl, likely burst forth and rip throats out before laying them in front of her as an offering.

For the next hour, I helped her shop, looking over the list she had, picking only the best fruits and vegetables, even though they were not for her. The primal need to only get her the best was strong in me, my basic animalistic urges to take care of my mate strong and growing stronger by the day.

And the entire time, my gaze lingered on my mate's perfection. Gods, I was so fucking lucky.

We left and started walking past the little stalls in the village. She stopped at one that had hand carved wooden figurines. This small smile played across her lips as she ran a finger over one, and then I noticed when she stilled before reaching out and touching the wolf figurine. The artists had painted the eyes a vibrant blue... just like my Lycan's... just like her eyes. Her brows were pulled down low, but then she seemed to shake herself out of her thoughts.

"What is it?" Although I knew. I knew she was feeling some kind of recognition, a connection. There was no way she wasn't, with me standing right beside her, the pheromones moving between us and only growing stronger with each passing moment.

"It's nothing," she whispered. "It's just," she said and glanced at me before emoting once more. "My neighbor, Mini, the older woman who I'm shopping for today, said something strange about me being here for a reason, something about wolves, but that they aren't really wolves." She shook her head and stopped, giving me a forced smile. "It's all kind of crazy."

*But it feels so real*, I could almost hear her say out loud.

"I just feel this weird connection to this place." She looked around, and a genuine smile covered her pink, full lips. "As soon as I stepped foot in this country, I just felt like—"

"—you were meant to be here," I finished for her.

She looked at me, and her smile widened. "Yes, exactly. Crazy, right?"

I shook my head, knowing my expression was serious. "We all have destinies, and sometimes those are fated with another." *Too fast. Don't push her.*

The way she watched me—this knowing look in her eyes—made me think she knew exactly what I meant, that she wouldn't deny this attraction between us.

"You speak like you've lived a thousand lives."

*Ah, sweetling, if only you knew how long I've waited for you.*

As we walked past the stalls, I marveled at the wonder on her face as she looked at the handmade pottery, the woven tapestry, the stitched folk dresses. Although she didn't speak Romanian, she knew a few words, thanking the stall owners, murmuring *beautiful, lovely,* and a handful of other sweet things to them in passing in my native tongue.

We rounded the corner, and I turned my attention to a stall that sold intricately handwoven silk scarves. I picked up a vibrant blue one, the same shade as Mikalina's eyes, and didn't hesitate to purchase it for her. When I was finished and the scarf wrapped in delicate tissue, I saw two men making their way toward my female, their vile lust clear on their faces as they let their eyes roam up and down her form.

*Destroy them for daring to look at her.*

My Lycan seethed the words, and I found myself moving toward them with pure violence building. Just a look from the opposite sex toward a mate would send my kind into a frenzied rage. But to know they desired what was mine? I'd tear their limbs from their bodies before they could even contemplate what I was doing.

She was unaware of their lewd looks as she picked up a piece of fresh fruit and brought it to her nose to smell.

I inserted myself between Mikalina and the duo, and they came to a stop, their eyes widening as they took note of me. I knew my eyes glowed blue, felt my muscles become bigger, adrenaline pumping through my veins in anticipation for a fight.

*Protect her. She's ours!*

I was breathing harder and faster, holding myself back, because I wanted to warn them, to see if they'd be smart enough to leave well enough alone... to leave with their lives intact.

They crossed themselves as if I were the very devil himself, and maybe I was. To them, I'd be whatever I needed to protect my mate.

They scurried off, and I closed my eyes and breathed out slowly, trying to rein myself in.

"Everything okay?" Mikalina's soft voice pierced through my red rage, and I exhaled once more, letting the fight leave me fully.

When I turned around, I was myself once again, gave her a smile that I was sure didn't reach my eyes, but held out the tissue-wrapped scarf to divert her worry.

"For me?" Her eyes were wide as she took the gift. She unwrapped it then made a small, surprised sound. "It's beautiful." She ran her fingers over the embroidered detailing around the edging.

"It's the same shade as your eyes."

"It's the same shade as my eyes." She snapped her head up and gave a small laugh as we said the same thing. "Thank you for this. I've never gotten anything so beautiful before."

I felt my brows lower. I didn't like that. I wanted to lavish things on her, spoil her, give her so much attention she was drowning in it. "It's nothing," I played it off. She'd soon realize, once she was mine, she'd never want for anything ever again.

We stayed in the market a short while longer, then I led her back through the woods. The conversation was easy, with her soft laughter having my body tightening, hardening in all the ways a man did for a woman. Before she knew it, I'd led her back to Dobravina. She seemed startled and surprised, but I planned this all along, refusing to leave even a moment of time spent with her wasted.

"Thank you," she said softly. "You've made this day... memorable."

My heart raced, my canines tingling to make it even more memorable for the both of us.

"How strange we just met, yet I feel like I've known you forever." The way she spoke was soft, absent, and as her eyes widened, I realized she hadn't meant to say those words out loud.

"Will you have dinner with me tomorrow?" I asked before she could say anything, before she could try to shake this fated feeling she had within her.

My focus was on her lips, and I couldn't help myself from feeling that gut-punch of arousal slam into me. There was no denying it or stopping it.

With the glow from the setting sun behind her, and her gorgeous face tipped up to look at me, the need to kiss her was so fucking strong. I curled my fingers into my palms and breathed out slowly, my nails turning into claws as I started to shift.

"Okay," she said almost breathlessly, no hesitation in her voice, and fuck did that make me even harder.

And when she lowered her eyes to my lips, I realized I was growling, the animal breaking free slightly. But she either didn't hear the low rumble, or she was too caught up in the moment, because she didn't react.

"I find myself," she murmured, still staring at my lips, and I lifted a hand and brushed away a strand of hair that blew gently across her cheek from the wind, "wanting to know more about you, to spend more time with you, Ren." She closed her eyes, and her breath caught when my skin touched hers.

*So receptive.*

"And you will."

She opened her eyes, and I saw the blue become brighter from her emotions... her arousal.

Yes, she would be mine. When the full moon hit, I was claiming my mate once and for all.

And I just hoped it didn't have her running from me forever.

## Mikalina

Ren picked me up just ten minutes ago, pulling up to the cottage in a sleek, dark, definitely luxury car. He'd been climbing out as soon as I stepped outside, and I could see a little bit of disappointment on his face as I hadn't waited for him. I knew it was because he wanted to come to the door and help me to the car, like the old-world gentleman I felt he was.

But now as I sat in the passenger seat, looking at the smooth interior, the scent of leather filling my nose, I couldn't help but feel very *aware* of him.

As in... embarrassingly aroused just by his presence.

The night was a bit chilly, and he turned the heater on, the warm gust of air moving across my knees. I didn't know if I should dress up for dinner, even though we were going to his house, so I'd gone casual and kind of regretted that decision now.

I glanced over at him, the lights from the dashboard illuminating his masculinity, seeming to make him even more handsome, if that was possible. He wore dark slacks that encased his big, muscular thighs perfectly. He wore a light-gray cashmere sweater, and underneath that, I could see a white dress shirt, the color crisp as it peeked out from underneath the collar, the bottom hem, and at the cuffs of his sweater.

*God, a man shouldn't look that good in clothing.*

I could only imagine how he'd look completely naked.

*Hard. Muscular. Golden skin. So much power.*

I snapped my head forward, my cheeks feeling hot at the images of what he might look like with nothing on. I shifted on my seat, clenched my thighs together, and tried to tell myself this was dinner and not the start of a one-night stand.

And then of course thinking about sleeping with him just made my desire even worse.

Looking out the passenger side window, I closed

my eyes and breathed out slowly. The arousal I felt for him had been growing steadily over the last day. And it was insane to think I felt this out of control in my desire for a man I'd just met twenty-four hours ago.

But there was no denying it.

Ever since he'd taken me to the village and walked me back home, I felt the lust uncoiling inside me, as if it had been dormant this whole time, as if it had always been deep within me my entire life and he'd been the key to unlocking it.

And now being so close to him, smelling the addicting and concentrated scent of his masculinity, a dark and spicy aroma that had me embarrassingly wet between my thighs, I idly worried that maybe I wouldn't be able to sit through an entire meal without eventually embarrassing myself.

This low rumble started in the interior, and at first I thought it was the engine, but when I looked over at Ren, I realized the noise was coming from him.

It was this deep vibration spilling out of his chest and filling the interior of the car.

My heart sped up, my palms started to sweat, and my nipples hardened.

He glanced at me then, his nostrils flaring as if

he were scenting me. His eyes were hooded, and I couldn't help but picture him looking like this in the throes of passion.

His expression was almost severe, animal-like in its intensity. It sent a shiver up my spine. And then it was my turn to feel chills racing up my arms and legs, and I forced myself to look away, the breath getting sucked from my very lungs just from that look he had in his eyes.

*I swear it's as if he can smell my arousal.*

I offered a smile that I knew didn't reach my eyes, but that smile faded at the pure look of... desire on his face. And just as he faced forward again, I swore I saw his eyes flash blue.

Pulling my brows down low, I chalked it up to a trick of the light and shadows and cleared my throat, needing to talk about something else to keep my mind off *other things*.

"So, you've lived here your whole life?" I heard him shifting on the seat and glanced over. His jaw was tight, a muscle clenching under his golden flesh.

A flash of heat slammed into me, and I bit my lip, thinking of extremely inappropriate things where Ren was concerned. His jaw clenched again and again, his hands tightening on the steering wheel, his knuckles white from the force.

What would he think if he knew I wanted him this badly? *What will he think, knowing—even though I'm a virgin—I'd give every part of myself to him tonight if he asked?*

Just the very thought of being with Ren in *that* way had the breath leaving me.

"I've lived here my whole life. Yes." His voice sounded strained, as if he forced himself to get the words out.

"Have you traveled out of the country much?" The conversation was being led into weird territory now, random questions that popped into my head, because I was desperately trying to steer my brain in another direction that was safe.

But even I knew it was pointless. Fruitless. I wanted him too much.

More shifting on the seat from him, and I lowered my gaze to his tree-trunk-sized thighs, my eyes growing wide as I noticed a very prominent bulge laying against his thigh and pressing against the fabric of his slacks.

Another clearing of his throat before he said, "I've traveled extensively over the years, but my home has always been here." The steering wheel creaked a little, and a moment later, he rolled down the window.

The cool air rushed in, and I shivered, but it had nothing to do with the sudden chill in the interior, and everything to do with the man sitting next to me.

"But I haven't traveled in a very long time, staying close because of my brother."

Once again, I felt a pang of sadness for him and for the man I'd never met.

"And you?"

"I haven't been anywhere outside of the US, not since before I took this trip."

He glanced at me with a surprised expression on his face. "And how are you enjoying your time in a foreign land?"

I smiled genuinely. "My time in each country has been incredible. I have learned so many new things, experienced different cultures I'd only ever dreamed of." I left out the part about how I enjoyed my time in Romania the most... because I'd met him.

Ren was by far my most enjoyable reason for taking this leap in life.

And given the fact that we'd just met yesterday, it seemed like admitting that to him now would be just the thing to send someone running in the other direction.

"I'm glad." He cleared his throat again, the wind softly blowing in the car still. "I'm glad you decided to come here for your trip."

I smiled again, even blushed. God, what was it about this man that made me feel so alive?

It was only another ten minutes driving and then Ren was pulling into his stately driveway and up to the massive home. I had a feeling he'd taken the long way to get here, but I didn't mind. And as I looked at him as he pulled the luxury car to a stop and cut the engine, I knew I wanted to see how far things could go with him. I wanted to experience things with Ren I'd only ever fantasized about.

"Shall we?" he asked and looked at me.

I nodded and went to open the car door, but his hand on my knee stilled me. My heart started racing, my breathing quickening. And all from that small touch. It was like fire on my body.

"Please, allow me?"

I licked my lips and nodded. This man was very old school. And I liked it.

He was out of the car and moving around the front of the vehicle, his big body causing my breath to come in short pants. He was just so... fearsome in appearance.

I spent some time with Mini today before Ren picked me up, and I wanted to ask her about Ren, but given the language barrier, and with Andrei still in the city, I was at a dead end. But as I'd been looking toward the forest, no doubt having this faraway look in my eyes because I'd definitely been daydreaming about Ren, I caught her gaze on mine. She had this knowing smile on her face as she murmured soft words in her native tongue.

He led me up the cobblestone walkway, the feel of his big hand on my lower back more arousing than it probably should've been.

And then we were inside, and I was frozen as I looked around at the opulence, at the hand carved wood accents, the detailing... the *everything*.

"God, Ren..." My words trailed off as I walked around. A gorgeous wide staircase was directly across from the double front doors. "It's magnificent." The flooring was also hardwood, polished, and a deep, rich brown color. There were exposed beams above, and the second story walls showed the same stone that graced the exterior of the home. I took note there were wolf details throughout the wood accents, large, violent animals with snarling jaws and aggressive stances. Yet they were also devastatingly beautiful.

He hadn't responded, so I glanced at him and saw his attention was wholly on me. I swallowed at how much I *felt* that look.

"It pleases me to no end that you like this home."

I shivered at the tone of his voice, sweet and thick and being poured over me in the most delicious of ways.

"Will you give me a tour?"

His smile told me I'd all but made his day, and when he held his arm out like a gentleman, I slipped mine through his and let him show me around.

And the entire time, I felt the strangest way about being here.

I felt like I was *home*.

CHAPTER

# SIXTEEN

**Ren**

I'd given my mate a proper tour of the manor —of the home I built for *her*. To know she enjoyed it, that it pleased her immensely, had pride swelling my chest. I'd taken my time showing her as much as I could before I felt her hunger, and my need to provide for her overrode anything else.

And here we were, dinner finished, my mate seated across from me, the whole atmosphere lethargic in the best way... in the way that told me she was satiated by her meal and her surroundings.

And I could smell her desire.

She was confused by it, a scent in my nose that tingled. She didn't understand why she felt this undeniable and extreme pull toward me. I knew that, even though she didn't speak the words out loud.

Mikalina was unsure why her body softened toward me without so much as a touch from me. She wondered why she was aroused, her pussy soaked and sensitive—something I could very much smell with approval. She kept squirming on the chair, her little nipples hard as diamonds under her top.

*Christ*, just thinking about her being primed for me, ready to let me claim her—my need to mark her —under the full moon, had me nearly snarling, baring my canines. I let my gaze drop to her throat, stared at the slender, pale column of her neck. My mouth watered to pierce her flesh, to let my Lycan canines slide right into her skin, leaving my mark so all males of my species would see whose mate she was.

*Mine.*

My body started reacting on its own once more for what felt like the hundredth time since seeing her just days ago. My chest rose and fell as I tried to take more oxygen into my lungs. My heart was beating harder to pump more blood through my veins. My nails started turning into claws, my body getting bigger, my Lycan rising to the surface as preparation to take the only woman who would ever satiate me.

I'd waited years—centuries—for her, for the moment when I'd part her thighs and slide into her, fill her up, make her take every single part of me. And in return, I'd take all that she had to offer.

She'd never have to want for anything, never have to worry about who would protect and provide for her, who would keep her safe.

That was my job, my pleasure, my honor.

She sat across from me, the table seeming even longer than it was. I needed her closer, wanted her on my lap, feeding from my hand. A low growl erupted from me, and I saw the way her eyes widened.

I sent the staff home after we finished our meal and they served dessert. I wanted to be alone with my female, even if technically we weren't really alone, not with a Lycan slowly going mad in the basement.

"Did you enjoy your meal?" I tried to keep my voice level, but it was deep, harsh from my arousal, and I could tell it affected her by the way she shifted on her seat. The fire behind me crackled as the flames licked over the wood.

"Everything was incredible. Thank you for

tonight." She brought her hand up and curled her tiny fingers around the stem of her wine glass, bringing the crystal to her lips and taking a long pull of the red alcohol. I noticed her hand slightly shook, her emotions and the sensations moving through her pronounced.

My cock throbbed behind the fly of my slacks, and I reached down to discreetly adjust it, although all that did was make me gnash my teeth from the short contact. When she set the wine glass down, I realized she downed the whole thing. I felt a smile form on my lips. "Another?" I gestured to the crystal, then to the bottle sitting in the center of the table.

"I better not." Already, her cheeks were pink, her breathing a little increased. She'd had two glasses, and I could see it already affected her.

I tilted my head and picked up my glass, finishing off my bourbon. I really shouldn't be drinking, not when liquor did nothing but inflame my senses even more, and with Mikalina right here, the scent of her desire for me growing by the second, that was a dangerous combination.

I tried to start light conversation, attempting to make her more relaxed, but she seemed tense, and the scent of her confusion, and the fact that she was trying in vain not to let her desire for me consume her, only made me want her more. Which seemed an impossible feat as it was.

"Look at me, Mikalina," I coaxed in a deep voice meant to stroke along her senses. She lifted her head, her pupils dilated, her lips redder from the increased blood flow. "Tell me what you want, and it's yours." I leaned forward, anticipating her response, holding my breath for her.

For long seconds, she didn't say anything, just licked her lips and smoothed her finger along the bottom of the wine glass. "I can't," she whispered.

My heart thundered at those two words. "No?"

She slowly shook her head.

"Just say the words." My voice was a husky purr now, one that I hoped had any reservations she felt vanishing.

Her chest rose faster and harder the longer we stared at each other.

"It's too soon."

I groaned, not even holding off the sound. "Too soon for what, sweetling?"

"To want the things I want... with you."

I curled my hands around the edge of the pine table, my nails digging into the wood, the force causing a loud creak to sound. I could have snapped the fucking table in half right now.

*To want the things I want... with you.*

Ah gods, she was killing me with her innocence.

"Come here, my female." I didn't hide the roughness in my voice, didn't try to pretend I wasn't an animal. I didn't even censor my endearment, didn't bother stopping those proprietary words, and Mikalina didn't correct me on it. I assumed maybe she'd instinctively—from her human side—tell me she wasn't mine. I would have told her otherwise, over and over again, that she was, in fact, *all mine*.

And when she stood without any hesitation, when she came forward, I all but purred in pleasure and approval.

Mikalina stood before me, and the very sight and smell of her had my eyes dropping to half-mast, had my body tightening further, and caused my cock to thicken impossibly more. The massive, thick length dug against the zipper of my slacks, and I didn't try to adjust it. Tonight wasn't about claiming her. No, that would be done on the full moon, when I was at my highest, most concentrated animal form, when there would be no stopping us... when she'd be just as frenzied and mindless with need for me as I would be for her.

And it would happen. I could smell her desire

pouring off of her, this sweetness that saturated the air and made me drunk from it.

I let my gaze linger along her face, then was shamelessly looking her over. I took in the delicate arch of her collarbones, went lower still to watch how her breasts rose and fell under the thin material of her shirt. My mouth dried at how hard her nipples were, the peaks stabbing through the shirt as if seeking my mouth.

And still, she stood there, knowing I was checking out every perfectly curvy inch of her, letting me have my fill.

Her eyes were hooded, her pupils dilated. *Sweet Jesus*, she was so aroused right now.

My cock throbbed again and again and again. The fucker jerked once more, the tip getting wet with pre-cum, the prelude to the massive explosion I'd no doubt have as I came and filled her up.

"What are you thinking about?" she asked softly, her voice huskier from her desire, although I gave her credit for trying to act like she wasn't just as affected in this moment as I was.

I let my gaze travel back up her body until I was looking in her eyes. "I'm thinking about when I first saw you, something in me awoke." I let those words hang between us. I wanted to tell her who I was to her, what she was to me, and the fact that she'd never be without me.

The need to explain about my Lycan side—my animal as much a part of me, maybe even more, as my human side. The words were on the tip of my tongue to explain that although I wasn't immortal, I lived centuries upon centuries, and that once I gave her my bite, she'd stop aging, never growing old until the time I faded away and went back to the earth. It was the way of my kind. She needed to know this before I claimed her, because Christ, I needed her to consent to this wholly.

I needed her to tip her head to the side and bare her throat, knowing what she was asking for, knowing she'd experience a world unlike she'd ever dreamed.

And no, I wouldn't think about her denying me. I wouldn't worry about her running from me. I'd give chase, of course. Always. But I'd never force her. I'd just keep trying, and trying, and trying.

*I want to tell her she'll never be alone, that she'll always have a protector.*

"You're just for me, all for me, female." I let my gaze linger on her lips, so soft and red and full. "I won't let anyone else have you. Never." I knew how possessive those words were, and they were the truth. Even if she denied me, told me she didn't want the mating—which would be the hardest, most devastating thing I'd ever experience in my long life—I'd never let another have her. I'd destroy any male who thought they could touch her, have what was mine.

And Mikalina would always be mine.

She gasped, maybe from my blunt honesty, maybe because she felt that truth deep in her soul.

"The instant I saw you"—*smelled the sweet scent of knowing you were my mate, an aphrodisiac the likes of which I'll ever experience from another*—"I knew I had to have you." *Because you were already mine, female.* "Something that called to me in the most primordial way." *You were made for me and me alone. The same as I am for you.* "You make me feel alive, Mikalina."

She stepped closer as if she couldn't stop herself, and I groaned in approval, coaxing her closer.

"I've never felt anything like that, and I knew I couldn't ignore it." *All because we are meant to be together.*

I didn't stop myself from lifting my arm and smoothing a finger over her bottom lip. She made a sweet, soft sound of pleasure.

"Tell me you feel that way too." I stared at her

mouth, wanting to kiss her, nip at the bottom swell, stroke my tongue between her lips.

"It's true," she gasped, and I gently pulled her bottom lip down, the flesh so very soft under my thumb, like silk and velvet, and everything else that was pleasurable to the touch. "It's crazy," she moaned, and her eyelids fluttered down.

*It's fate, my darling.*

She moved another step closer, and I snagged her around the waist and had her on my lap seconds later, her legs straddling either side of my thighs. It was my turn to close my eyes in pleasure. The feel of her on top of me, the hottest, most intimate part of her right up against the hardest, thickest part of me, nearly having me coming right then. I rolled my hips up involuntarily, grinding my cock against her, and she gasped, pressing down.

*Gods. Yes.*

"There isn't anyone or anything that'll ever keep me from you." I should've censored my words, knowing I might scare her away, push her, cross lines. She wasn't from my world, maybe knew nothing about the supernatural. She probably thought it was all in books and movies, not real, big, breathing, and currently holding her close. "Does that frighten you?" I could smell she was still very much aroused. There was no fear, no worry... nothing but, dare I fucking say... acceptance?

She wanted me more than she wanted to worry about how fast this was moving, or how confused she felt because she was so drawn and connected to me.

And when she slowly shook her head, staring into my eyes, I looked at her mouth again, knowing she could feel how hard my entire body got. I wasn't tensing from the shock of her accepting me and this. I was hardening because my Lycan was so close to the surface.

And when she gasped, I knew she'd seen my eyes change color, the whiskey shade morphing briefly to the blue of my inner beast.

"Your eyes," she whispered, and I closed them and shook my head.

"It's nothing," I assured her and only opened them when I felt I was more in control. "Don't worry about them." But fuck, I was losing this battle, and I knew they flashed right back to blue the moment I locked gazes with my mate.

Her brows furrowed, and then she shook her head, closing her eyes and exhaling slowly.

"What is it?" I asked gently, coaxing her to share anything with me, because I was starved for it, hungry for every little piece of information about my female.

"It's silly," she whispered and opened her eyes again.

"Nothing you have to say would be construed as that to me. I assure you."

She gave me a ghost of a smile, her fingers curling slightly on my shoulders. I gritted my teeth to hold off my desire. "It's just that Mini, the owner of the cottage I'm renting, spoke about these creatures in the woods with glowing blue eyes." She lifted her hand and ran a finger right below her own blue eyes—ones the same shade as my Lycan's.

My heart was racing now, the truth on her lips, but she thought it nothing more than fable.

"It's silly. I know. Wolf-like creatures roaming the woods of Romania, these animals that are part-man, part-wolf, living in the Carpathian Mountains."

*If only you knew, my female. But you soon will, and I fear I'll frighten you so badly you'll run from me.*

"Sometimes, the truth in this world is far stranger than what we could ever imagine."

Her vision cleared as she stared into my eyes. "Yes," she murmured, then placed her fingers on my cheek. "I feel myself focusing on other things though... things that may not make sense." Her brows dipped low again before she slowly shook her head. "I feel this... connection with you, Ren, one that makes me not want to question anything, because this all feels so right." She was looking into my eyes now, her arousal climbing higher as her mind pushed away everything else but this moment with me.

*Yes. Gods, yes, Mikalina. The same as I feel for you.*

# SEVENTEEN

### Ren

"Please tell me it's not just me," Mikalina whispered, maybe to herself.

I wound my arms tighter around her, needing her closer. Gods, I needed her so much closer. I needed us fused, irrevocably tied together for all of eternity. "I've known you were mine before you even came into my life, *iubirea mea*." I knew my words would make no sense, and I wanted so desperately to tell her what she really was to me.

*Patience.*

"What does that mean?" she asked softly, her body warming for me further. I could smell the heat of her, the arousal slowly growing like a fire from kindling.

I pushed her hair away gently, lingering on the smooth, soft, and warm expanse of where her throat met her shoulder. I couldn't help but let my gaze focus on that area... right where my bite would go.

My mouth watered, my canine incisors elongating in preparation.

*Patience.*

"My love, or something to that extent," I murmured, my focus still on that sweet spot at her neck. My cock was so hard, thick and long, and I couldn't help but roll my hips, knowing I was digging the fucker against her.

She gasped and tightened her nails into my arms, holding on, but also pressing down on me.

I tipped my head back slightly as a shot of ecstasy slammed into me. My eyes dropped to half-mast, my gaze trained on her eyes, seeing she was getting to that moment right with me... the one where she was so fucking primed she couldn't think straight.

I kept my mouth closed so she wouldn't see my fangs, so she wouldn't see how much my mouth watered to pierce her flesh and give her my mark.

*Patience.*

"That's one hell of an endearment," she whispered, and when I lifted my hips again, pressed my cock against her core, she closed her eyes and moaned, gripping me tighter, her words trailing off.

I wanted her... badly. I desired her more than I'd ever desired anything in my long existence, and here she was—my mate—for the taking.

"I feel... like I'm burning alive, Ren."

I had my mouth at her throat after she uttered those words, my lips and tongue lashing at her flesh. I groaned at her sweetness, the flavor of her skin exploding on my tongue. She was an aphrodisiac. Everything about her was so potent to me I knew I'd never get enough. I'd continue to crave and crave and crave her until I drew my last breath. My need for Mikalina would only grow with each passing day.

"I need to feel you, touch you... taste you." I pulled back, a feat hard as fuck. "Will you let me, my female?"

She opened her eyes and looked at me with a drugged expression. I didn't censor my verbiage, even knowing she might think it was weird the words I said. *My female. My love.* I hoped she thought it was because of a language barrier, English as my second language, so my words sounded strange to her. She could think that right now. It would make things easier for her mind. But eventually—very fucking soon—she'd know the truth of what they meant.

"Will you let me make you feel good?"

Gods, she was breathing so hard, her eyes so blue they almost glowed from her desire.

"This is so crazy," she murmured and lowered her eyes to my lips. "But I can't seem to say no to you." She looked back into my eyes. "I don't want to say no to anything with you, Ren."

I let out a purr of approval and rolled my hips again, loving how she gasped from the contact.

"I'm so confused," she said and looked at my mouth once more. "But I don't even care, because I want you too much, Ren."

I growled, fucking growled like the Lycan I was.

In a matter of seconds, I cleared the table in front of me with a sweep of my arm and had Mikalina sitting on the smooth wood, her legs spread, her eyes wide. While staring into her shocked but pleasure-hazed expression, I gripped her ankles and placed her feet on the edge of the table. She wore pants, but they were no match for my passion. I'd tear them away like they were tissue.

"You want this?"

She licked her lips and nodded.

I was barely hanging on as it was, and the scent of her arousal slammed into my nose, making me sway in my chair, having my whole body ache for more. "Trust me to take care of you, Mikalina. Trust me to make this good for you." Gods, I felt like another male, like someone else occupied my body.

*Something does.* This beast. This feral creature, that was by all accounts stronger than anything else on the planet, was clawing to get out.

It wanted this female too.

With my hands on her ankles, I spread my palms upward, holding her gaze with mine. When my fingers were perilously close to her core, she let her head fall back on her neck, closed her eyes, and breathed out slow and long.

"*Ren,*" she moaned.

I snapped, letting my nails lengthen to claws and tearing at her pants until they were nothing but shreds of fabric scattered around the table and floor.

She snapped her head up and gasped, looking at the remains of her pants. But I could see she liked this erotic violence, this act of need so strong in me that I had no control over myself.

I kept my hands out of her view so she couldn't see my claws, and while still holding her eyes with mine, I leaned forward. Her scent was even more saturated with only a thin pair of cotton panties blocking her sex from me, and I closed my eyes and groaned. Her heat swirled around me, sucking the energy from the very pit of my soul. Gods, if this was how I died, there'd be nothing better in the world.

I ran the tip of my nose up her center, feeling how wet she was, the material soaked clean through.

"My female is hungry for me." I didn't expect her to respond... not unless she gave me her answer by moaning and spreading her thighs wider.

Which she did.

"Ren... oh yes. God. Ren, yes."

I kissed her gently, inhaled her deeply. I couldn't get enough. I gripped the edge of her panties and in one swift move tore the thin material away. And as I looked at her perfection, stared between her thighs, I grew dizzy from my lust.

Pink. Swollen. Wet.

So... fucking wet.

"The sooner you realize you're mine, the easier this will be." I shouldn't have said it. Then again, I didn't. My Lycan was pushing forward, breaking through my control every now and again, taking over so he could experience this as well.

I lowered my focus from her face to her chest, watching as her breasts rose and fell violently under her shirt. I snapped my attention back at her face. "Admittedly, I like the chase. I crave your resistance, because that means your surrender will be all the sweeter."

A small noise left her.

"You're so wet for me, my female."

She made a small noise in the back of her throat and looked into my face.

Wide, aroused eyes.

Blown-out pupils.

Increased breathing.

Pulse beating rapidly at the base of her throat.

"More," she moaned softly, her lips parting in pleasure.

My arms were locked tight, the muscles straining, my need to control myself a razor's edge. I moved my fingers down her inner leg, right beside her pussy, and then didn't torment us any longer. I touched her pussy lips lightly, spreading my fingers through her soaked slit. I couldn't stop from groaning.

"Yeah," I said to myself low, huskily. "My tiny female wants this, and I'm eager to satiate her."

"God. Ren. Yes, yes, I want this."

And that was all I needed for any remaining control I had to fucking snap right in two.

I slipped a hand under her so I could place it on the small of her back, then moved my other onto her belly, keeping her in place as I started to lick at her cleft, sucked on her clit, and groaned as I savored her flavor.

"Watch me," I growled in a voice that wasn't from my human side. It was rough and sharp around the edges. "Look at what I'm doing, how I'm drinking your honey, letting all that sweetness slip down my throat."

She lifted her head, her lips parting, a soft moan leaving her as her gaze locked between her thighs at what I was doing to her.

I ran my tongue up and down her slit, giving her so much ecstasy I knew she'd always crave me... just like I'd always need her. My groans no doubt vibrated over her pussy. She was spread before me like an offering, a meal for me, something I could feast on until I was drowning in the flavor and scent of her.

I feasted on her, knowing I'd never get enough, and when she came for me, her back arching, her hands thrust into my hair as she tugged at the strands, I growled, letting my Lycan rise up momentarily to experience this right along with me.

*Mine.*

*Ours.*

*Yes. Claim her now. Now!*

It was long seconds before I finally stopped lapping at her, leaning back and breathing like I'd been running for hours, my body super-aware of every little detail that made my mate. My gaze was riveted to the sight of her pussy, her legs spread wide, her knees falling all the way open. *So wet, even now.*

I finally tore my eyes from between her legs to see her staring at me. The way her eyes widened when she looked into mine told me how I appeared, told me the color was no longer brown in shade but blue and vivid from my Lycan.

I could feel myself start to change, my canines elongating, the twin points pressed to my lower lips. I knew my body probably appeared bigger, more muscular, and that if I lifted my hands, my nails would be long, dangerous claws.

But I couldn't help it, not when I was so fucking turned on, not when I *allowed* my animal to experience this small snippet of what it was like with our mate.

Her scent covered my mouth, surrounding me, and it was drawing me closer to a brutal start where I truly had no control. I was going to fucking lose it.

I pushed away from her, standing, pacing. I ran my hands over my arms, up and down, up and down. I closed my eyes and just breathed, trying to stem off the change, the shift that would terrify her.

"Ren?" She said my name in this frightened tone.

I spun on her, my eyes now open, my breathing harsh.

She made an almost startled sound and scrambled to sit up before getting off the table and stumbling back from me. "Oh God," she whispered and covered her mouth with her hands. I turned from her, giving her my back as I tried to control myself. "What are you?" Her voice shook, and I heard the rustling of clothing as she no doubt dressed.

Although the need to take her right now was strong in me, my arousal was doused with the revelation of what was about to transpire, and the fact that my mate feared me. I closed my eyes, breathing out. I was shocked though that she hadn't ran out of here screaming.

"What are you?" she asked again, and I exhaled.

This moment was bound to come, especially since I had no intentions of letting her go, but I hadn't meant for her to be frightened. I wanted to ease her into it, although I'd run out of time.

"I'm not human, not wholly. A Lycan, Mikalina."

She didn't answer for long seconds, and I wondered what was going on in that beautiful head of hers.

"You're saying you're some kind of wolf shifting person?" She sounded skeptical, maybe even hesitant, probably thinking I was a lunatic.

"I'm just another species in the *Otherworld*. Although I can shapeshift, so yes, I suppose lore got that right."

She was panting, her eyes wide, her confusion and fear so very real. "Another species," she murmured then glanced down and furrowed her brows. "*Otherworld*, as in supernatural other world... stuff?" My silence must have been confirmation enough because she let out a gust of air. "What else aren't you telling me?" Her voice was steady, her gaze even. "I know there's more," she whispered.

"I'm a Lycan. And you're my mate."

# EIGHTEEN

### Mikalina

L*ycan.*

*Able to shift into a wolf-like creature.*

*I'm his mate.*

Was I dreaming? I had to be, because this was the most fantastical—maybe even ridiculous—thing I'd ever experienced in my life.

I thought over and over again about what Ren just told me, my heart thundering, my body still awake from the intense pleasure he'd just given me. But not even this truth, this unbelievable reality, could douse the fire still simmering in me. And I felt like I was traitorous to myself for feeling this hard need for a man that wasn't really a man at all.

I exhaled, thankful he stayed by the fire and didn't make a move toward me. He seemed... *heartbroken* at having told me, knowing I was terrified. But as I stood there, I felt some of the shock start to leave. I felt reasoning and rationalization start to replace all the confusion.

*Another species.*

*Think. Think.*

"You're taking this better than I expected."

I snapped my head up to look at him. He was leaning against the wall, his arms crossed over his big, wide chest. *God, he looks so good.* I shook my head and told my thoughts to stay at the task at hand.

"I envisioned this going a lot differently."

I lifted a brow at that, and it was my turn to cross my arms. I tried to appear stronger than I felt, but I knew the act was all about protecting myself. "How did you envision it going?" My voice was surprisingly strong and clear.

"You running away and never looking back," he said matter-of-factly.

"I thought about it," I responded honestly. That had been my first inclination. But even if the fight instinct had been strong in me, I hadn't been able to leave. "I figure you're either batshit crazy, or... this is pretty damn real." I shook my head. "I contemplated running," I murmured and gave a humorless laugh.

"Why didn't you?"

I repeated what he said in my mind for long moments and came up with the only thing that made sense out of all of this. "Because it felt wrong to leave you."

He sucked in a breath, as if shocked by my words, and then I heard a low sound come from him, a mix between a growl and a purr. I looked at him, taking note of everything about him.

"As crazy as this entire situation is, I'm not all that surprised." I shook my head again at how freaking insane that sounded coming from my mouth. "I mean, the first time I saw you, I felt like you didn't seem like any other man I'd come across in my life." I licked my lips as that pleasure started to heighten once more. "You seemed inhuman, in a way. I guess I know why I felt like that."

He pushed away from the wall, and involuntarily I took a step back. "I won't hurt you. I'd never hurt you."

I swallowed. "I know."

He lifted an eyebrow. "So you believe me, understand what I am?"

*No. Yes.* "I don't know what I understand or

believe, but everything in me is screaming that you're telling me the truth, that you won't hurt me." I didn't bother bringing up the whole Mini story she told me. It wouldn't matter at the end of the day.

"Given what I am, how can you not assume I'm some crazed beast wanting to harm you?"

I shrugged half-heartedly. When he put it that way, I supposed I didn't know shit. But... "You've had plenty of time to do that if you'd meant to. And —" I nibbled my bottom lip. "—given what we just did, I can't see hurting me is your intention." My face felt hot as my pussy became wet once more at the memory of how good he made me feel.

He growled again, his head lowering slightly, his eyes becoming hooded as he stared at me.

"Can you..." I breathed out slowly, knowing I should feel embarrassed for what I was about to ask. "Can you smell my desire?" My voice was so low, breathy, but I knew he heard me anyway by the way he groaned.

"Oh *yes*." His voice sounded different, deeper, huskier, and his eyes kept flashing from blue to brown.

"Why do they do that?" I swallowed, this little part of me still saying I needed to run, that this wasn't normal or safe. But the much stronger part refused to leave him.

He closed his eyes, squeezing them as if grappling for control. When he opened them again, they were normal. "My inner animal pushes through at times, far more now that you're in my life. The blue coloring is his eye shade."

*It's the same as mine.* I didn't want to think too deeply on that, but then again, the fact that they were a perfect match just seemed to bring about the whole *mate* situation.

I cleared my throat, trying to focus on something other than the fact that even though things had definitely gone into the fucked up category, my body still hummed with arousal. "Are there more of you? Different species?"

He inclined his head, and I was taking that as a very old world, aristocratic gesture from him when he agreed with me. "Many. Hundreds."

"Vampires?" He nodded. "Witches and warlocks?" Ren inclined his head again.

"Demons too, but they are an aggressive bunch of bastards and thankfully keep to themselves most of the time." He took a step toward me, but I held my ground, even though I was still a little nervous about all this. "I hope to tell you about all the different kinds of creatures that make their homes amongst humans."

*I want that too.*

I swallowed and smoothed my hands down my thighs. "How old are you?"

He paused for a moment, and I was pretty sure what he was about to say would be another shock to my system.

"Over three centuries old."

And yup... the air went right out of my lungs, and I staggered back.

An over three-hundred-year-old werewolf... Lycan... whatever he called himself, was standing in front of me, claiming I was his mate.

"Do you live forever?"

He shook his head. "Some of the species in the supernatural world do possess immortality. My kind is not one of them. The oldest known supernatural is rumored to be over a millennium old, but we have our own folklore within the supernaturals, so I couldn't tell you if that's just rumor, what his species is, or if it is true if he's actually out there still."

I felt my eyes widen.

"Although I'll live far longer if I have my mate by my side."

I felt my brows lower at his use of that *mate* term again. "What does that mean when you say I'm your mate?" Did I *really* want to know this?

He exhaled and ran a hand over the back of his short, dark hair, then he turned and faced the fire. "I wanted to go slow with you. But I'm running out of time." The last part was muttered so low I wasn't quite sure I heard him clearly. But before I could ask, he faced me again. "I have one female born to be mine and mine alone." He stared at me right in the eyes as he let that sink in.

I swallowed, knowing this was fucking insanity, but another part of me felt like what he said couldn't be anything but the truth. I *felt* something the moment I'd seen him, this pull, a weird connection that was undeniable. Could what he said actually be the truth, actually make sense? Or was I allowing myself to be pulled down to some crazy world where this man needed to get professional help.

But his eyes. The size of him. The way he seemed so... *not* human.

"And if I... don't want to be your mate?" It felt so very wrong to even utter those words. It was physically painful to say them, like acid being poured down my throat. I noticed how tense he became after I said it, as if the very thought of me not wanting to be his was too unbearable. "What if you don't want *me* as a mate—"

"Not possible," he cut me off. "You were made for me and me alone." I swallowed at hearing those words again. He sounded so final. "There isn't any part of you that I don't find desirable above all else."

And there went my heart, just plummeting into my belly.

"And every part of me—especially my Lycan— wants to claim you, *Mikalina*," he growled my name, and I took a step back, sensing he was changing in this moment, becoming more primal, animalistic.

"What happens when you claim me?" That question was barely a breath from my lips, but I found myself desperate to know the answer.

"If I told you, I'd frighten you by the intensity."

"Tell me," I breathed out.

A moment of silence stretched, before he growled out, "I'd become more animal, my canines lengthening in preparation to bite you, mark you." He was breathing harder—the same as I was—as if speaking these words turned him on. And I was shocked to find they were arousing me. "My nails would lengthen to claws, my body becoming taller, bigger."

"Would you turn into a wolf?" My voice was so breathless. Oh my God, was I actually entertaining any of what he said?

He growled low but shook his head. "I'd never fully change when I took you."

*When he* took *me.*

That sounded so erotic.

"But it's getting harder and harder, Mikalina, to stop myself from making you mine." He took a step closer, his eyes flashing blue. "My beast wants you so fucking much." His voice didn't sound normal. "And the full moon is coming, teasing me, tempting me. It's the one time I'll let him dominate... because he wants *you.*"

I took another step back, shaking my head, afraid of what he said, confused... needing it like I needed to breathe. I closed my eyes and ran my hands over my face, feeling like the world had just opened up and swallowed me whole.

"I should probably go." I was surprised I could say anything in that moment. I let my hands fall from my face and looked at Ren again.

He stayed back, thankfully giving me the space I desperately wanted right now. I could see on his face he didn't want that, but he didn't try to talk me into staying, and didn't come any closer either. And for that, I was glad. I needed some time to think. I needed to understand what exactly happened tonight.

*I need to calm down from the intense pleasure he gave me.*

It took several moments of him breathing in and out slowly, as if trying to gather his bearings. "I understand, although I'd be lying if I said I don't want you to leave." His voice was still husky but sounded normal again.

My heart started speeding up at that, and as much as I didn't want to, I had to put some distance between us. "Yeah, I should go. I need to go."

"Will you let me walk you home?" Those words were tight as they came out of him, as if the very idea of me leaving him was painful, as if he were stopping himself from pouncing on me.

God, there was this man—this *non-human* man —being so kind and good, and had been like that from the very first moment I'd met him, but then he dropped this massive truth in my lap, one that sounded more like fantasy, and I was utterly confused. I wanted to just say, *yeah, I'm cool with all this. I just want you and nothing else matters.* But was I understanding any of this?

Right now... no; no, I wasn't understanding any

of this, and I think getting away from Ren would help, and that even meant just walking home. Maybe that was stupid, and maybe I should have been smarter and taken him up on his offer, because wild animals and shit. But being around him scrambled my brain, and right now, I needed to get it level.

I didn't know what else to say, so I started heading toward the front door. He didn't stop me, and I was thankful, because I wouldn't have had the willpower to deny him if he asked me to stay again.

Once the door was open and the cool breeze rushed over me, I looked over my shoulder and saw him standing in the same spot, his hands tucked into the pockets of his slacks, his gaze seeming very *wolfy* in that moment. A shiver skated over my skin, and I faced forward and left, shutting the door behind me.

And as I followed the trail back to town, the entire time I knew I wasn't really alone.

I knew Ren followed me in the shadows to make sure I got home safely.

### CHAPTER NINETEEN

**Mikalina**

*Several days later*

I'd stayed away for days, getting used to the idea of what Ren told me—or trying to, at least.

I had one opportunity to ask Mini—with Andrei as the interpreter—about Lycans, about Ren and the folklore she'd known as a child. But when the opportunity had risen, I found the idea of talking about Ren and what he told me... not my place. I felt proprietary of him, which was ludicrous in and of itself, given how long I'd known him. But telling that story—his story—felt wrong on every level.

So I said nothing, which gave me no additional answers to my many questions.

And now here I was, standing on the little stoop of the cottage, thinking about Ren and how no matter what reality and what I *thought* I'd known my entire life, I wanted him. I believed him.

*And I wanted to go to him.*

For the hundredth time, I thought about the folklore Mini told me about wolf-like creatures. About Ren's species. I *did* feel like I'd been drawn to this place. And as I stood here on the stoop and closed my eyes, I could feel the wind along my skin and hear the distant sound of birds nearby as if my senses were heightened.

*I don't want to ignore what I feel for Ren.*

There was more I needed to know, more from Ren, and I knew he'd give me the answers. I knew he *wanted* to. He'd given me the space I needed to think, and for that I was grateful.

And this whole time, not once did I think about leaving to go back to America.

I exhaled. I'd had no one to confide in, even if I wanted to. No close friends, not even parents who acted like they'd give a shit. They berated me for even wanting to take this trip, making me feel like I was some immature child who couldn't settle down.

"Lycan?" My voice trembled as I whispered that word, the one I'd been repeating in my head nonstop since leaving Ren.

Just then, I heard the sound of a door opening and closing, and a moment later, the soft footsteps of someone approaching. I glanced to my side to see Mini coming forward, her expression fierce amongst her wrinkled face. She said nothing as she stopped before me, watching me with such knowing eyes.

And then she spoke, soft, low words I couldn't understand. She held out her hand, and in the center of her palm was a tiny wooden wolf carving.

"Fate," she said in English, her accent thick. "Love."

I reached out with a shaking hand and took the little figurine, staring at it, wondering how she'd known this was my fate when I hadn't a clue. I'd always felt lost. *Until now.*

And when she gave me a grandmotherly smile and a pat on my arm, I felt warmth fill me, the kind that said everything would be okay if I just let it.

# TWENTY

## Ren

I tried to stay away, and did a pretty good job of it the last few days. But I knew once the moon was full—tonight—there was no stopping my Lycan from claiming Mikalina. The pull and need would be too hard to resist, the instinct driving all rational, humane thought from my mind until I was nothing but a ravenous animal for her.

I'd contemplated just leaving the country, getting as far away as I could before the full moon hit, but I knew that wouldn't even stop me.

I sat in front of the fire and nursed a whiskey, staring at the flames, this little ritual something I tended to do nightly, it seemed. But having a life expectancy that just went on and on and on made life monotonous—that was until I'd found my female.

The full moon pulled me, urged me, tempted and coaxed me. I fought it, had all day, feeling it slowly grow. And as the sun was starting to set, there was no denying what I'd do. But I'd chain myself up, if that's what it took. I would never force Mikalina into anything, never make her take my mating mark or the full moon claiming. But I had to lock myself away now or I wouldn't be able to. And even with chains all around me, holding me down, the threat of me breaking free with my inhuman strength to get to my mate was great.

I finished off my whiskey just as I felt a prickling along my skin. Then there were three hard knocks on the front doors. I knew who it was, felt her as if she stood right before me already. I was out of my seat and striding toward the entrance before I could even take a breath.

I opened the massive wood, the steel and wood creaking from the force, and as I stared at my female, nothing else mattered, because I knew her coming here had been a mistake.

*Won't be able to stop.*
*I will claim her.*
*And God help both of us.*

# TWENTY-ONE

### Mikalina

As soon as he opened the door, I felt a blast of heat, pleasure... need.

From Ren.

He stared at me with such intensity, his eyes flashing blue, reminding me of what he was, how he wasn't a human. He was something more, something other. I planned on having this full conversation with him, hashing out everything, trying to learn all that I could, but as soon as he opened the door, all I felt was this intense need for Ren. It pushed everything else out of my mind until there was only one thing that echoed.

*Want.*

*I want him. I need him. Let him take me.*

He looked down at my lips, and I found myself licking them involuntarily, as if his focus on them was like a tangible touch from his finger.

*This is crazy to want Ren when I know what he is... this supernatural creature that is straight from a fairy tale.*

"I'd rather die than ever hurt you," he murmured low as if to himself, the first thing to spill from his lips. His voice sounded pained, and my breath caught. "That's why you need to leave. You need to run. I'll lock myself away, but the farther you get from me, the better chance you have."

"Better chance of what?" Why was I so breathless?

"Mikalina," he groaned as if my very name turned him on. "You shouldn't have come."

There was a long moment of silence, but I waited. I came here for answers, for clarity, and I'd get it... eventually.

"When it's the full moon, I'm not myself. My inner animal has free reign. I'll become bigger, my nails turning to claws, my canines turning to fangs. The only thing I'll be mindful of is needing you, fucking you... marking your neck so everyone will know you're mine."

I shivered at the intensity of his words. He cupped my cheek and smoothed his finger over my flesh, and I couldn't help but lean into him.

"For my mate—for you—I'd die a thousand deaths just to make sure you weren't hurt and that you never feared me." He stared into my eyes intently. "And you will fear me, be frightened, terrified by what I'll become."

I found myself shaking my head, as if this man who I'd grown to care for over this last week didn't know himself like I did. Which was fucking insane. Clearly, he knew how hard the mating would be if he was warning me.

"You won't hurt me," I said, although how the hell could I even be sure?

*God, what in the hell am I getting myself into? Why am I not listening to him and fleeing, heading back to America and away from something that feels like it's been plucked right out of a story?*

Again, I thought of Mini's words about wolves and destinies, and I felt myself falling harder and faster for Ren.

Before I knew what was happening, or even processed my thoughts and how I truly felt, Ren added a bit of pressure to my face before leaning down and pressing his mouth to mine, as if he couldn't stop himself from reacting to me being close.

And I couldn't help but accept all he gave me... even if it was fucking insane.

When he stroked my lips with his tongue, my pussy clenched, my clit throbbed, and I felt a fresh rush of warmth and wetness settle between my thighs. His lips were firm, full, and the flavor of him was spicy, wild, and all for me. My body started to tingle, and I felt my heart start to jackknife behind my ribs. I wanted to touch him, but another part of me, maybe the common sense part—the survival part—told me this man was inherently dangerous.

*But not to me. Never to me.*

And I was listening to my inner voice, that gut feeling that told me this was *right*.

I gasped at the sensations moving through me, and he used that opportunity to dip his tongue into my mouth. I moaned at the flavor of him. It was a mix of alcohol and everything that was Ren.

Maybe it was the adrenaline pumping through my veins, or the fact that I couldn't deny there was hardcore arousal moving between us. All I knew was my emotions were high right now, and I didn't want to come back to reality.

I wanted to embrace whatever *this* was.

And so I curled my fingers around his massive biceps, knowing what I was allowing to happen was irrevocable. There was no going back.

And I didn't even care.

# TWENTY-TWO

**Ren**

My mate was so fucking soft against me. I was stunned that she came back, let alone was kissing me, letting me touch her... was wet for me. I inhaled her sweetness and growled at how perfect she smelled.

And when Mikalina touched my arms, curling her nails into my flesh to bring me even closer, my cock thickened even more, growing impossibly longer, bigger. I wanted her, more than anything I'd ever wanted in my entire life. I finally had my female and would give her all of me. She was my one and only. I'd saved myself for her for all these years, never desiring another, never even contemplating giving up on finding her and sharing my body with her and her alone.

I wanted my mark on her, wanted Mikalina by my side for all time. I wanted my young in her belly, and wanted her to admit she was mine irrevocably.

*No one will ever have her but us,* my Lycan purred. *She's ours. Our mate, and tonight, we'll claim her.*

I grabbed the back of her head at the same time I stroked her tongue with mine. But with each passing second she was in front of me, as the sun continued to set, the moon soon becoming full, the greater chance of her not getting away from me in time.

"I'll never let you go." It was my Lycan who spoke, although my human side felt the same way. But because the moon was coming up fast, he had more power.

She gasped against my mouth, no doubt *feeling* how proprietary those words were. I started walking us backward, the primal side of me taking control, roaring out to take her, to claim her, because she was my mate in every way.

The wall beside the double front doors stopped our movements, and I groaned against her mouth, my cock hard, demanding, and aching so much I didn't stop myself from grinding the thick length against her belly.

I broke away to breathe, to try to control myself. I was slowly losing my mind, and the scent of my mate—of her arousal for me—was going to bring me to my knees.

"Your eyes," she breathed out. "Ren, your canines... they're so sharp and long. God, your body is getting so much bigger right in front of me."

I closed my eyes and panted. "Mikalina," I ground out.

"Ren?" Her voice was hesitant but still filled with so much arousal. Gods, she was strong, stronger than I was.

I opened my eyes, my Lycan taking full control now.

There was no going back, and so I growled, "*Run.*"

# TWENTY-THREE

**Mikalina**

E verything in me screamed to go back to him, that this was supposed to happen, that I was supposed to be *his*. It was that voice that had me pushing away everything I'd always known about what was in the world, what life was made up of, and going to him, confronting this head on.

But he told me to run in a voice that was no longer his, distorted and deep, more of a growl than anything else.

So that's what I did. I ran.

I stumbled over fallen logs, branches whipping at my arms and face. I was no longer on the path, now stumbling forward, the darkness thick, but the glow from the moon high above was almost this calming balm.

I felt no pain as those leaves and branches swatted at me like hungry hands trying to stop me.

"So my female wants to run?" Ren's voice was low, deep, distorted as it moved around me. God, it sounded like he was in my head, like his words wrapped themselves around me, taunting me... teasing me.

I shook and moaned, chills racing over my body. I wanted him, yet I couldn't stop running.

*He loves the chase. He needs this. I need this.*

I knew the human side of him was gone, pure instinct riding him now. The feel of that silvery glow from the moon washed over me, and I moaned anew, as if that light bathed me in pure pleasure. *Oh God. What's happening?*

His wolf was right behind me. I sensed him, *felt* him chasing me.

And so I ran faster, tripping over my own feet, no longer running from the unknown, but running because I knew my mate was after me and would claim me.

And I wanted him to catch me.

I was too aroused, my legs feeling weak, my feet

sinking into the ground as if quicksand tried to pull me down, slow me for *him*.

The roar that sounded behind me had my heart racing in... anticipation for him reaching me.

"Run, my female. Run. But know I'll chase you, *mate*. I'll chase you until the end of the world. Know I love it, yearn for the catch." He growled erotically, and I could practically feel his warm breath on the back of my neck.

I heard hard rustling behind me, twigs snapping, trees being decimated in his wake, because of his wrath.

And I knew the moment he reached out and snagged me around the waist, pulling us down, taking the force so I wasn't crushed by his massive weight.

Before I could even make a sound or suck in a breath, his mouth was on mine, his hands working at my clothing, tearing it off.

"Tell me you accept me, you submit to me," he growled and kissed me. I wrapped my arms around his neck and arched my back, which made him become even more frenzied. "Tell me you'll always be mine, that you crave me as much as I do you." His voice was so serrated. "Tell me you yearn for my mark."

I gasped and opened my mouth wider, accepting his brutal kiss.

"Yes," I moaned, arching up against him again, letting him tear the clothes from my body. He kissed me with a violent passion I never knew I needed, with a passion that burned me from the inside out.

He stroked his tongue over my lips, forcing me to take it into my mouth, fucking me there like I needed him to do between my thighs. I could hear him snarling, growling, the vibrations doing wicked things to my pussy, making me yearn in a way I never imagined.

I was vaguely aware of our clothing in tatters around our bodies, the glow from the moon washing over us so elicit, so erotic, that I threw my arms above my head and fully stretched out under him.

He flexed and released his fingers on my hips, his claws digging into my flesh but not enough to hurt me. I knew that this encounter, this mating as he called it, would be so heated I wouldn't even be able to comprehend the magnitude of it.

I wouldn't know fully how permanent it was until it was said and done.

I knew without him having to say the words against my sensitive lips that he wanted me to surrender fully—totally—to him.

And God help me, but I wanted that too.

The fire running through my veins could not be ignored, couldn't be extinguished, and right now, I didn't want it any other way.

When Ren broke the kiss and started moving his lips down my face, as if he savored the flavor and feel of me, I closed my eyes and moaned. His tongue lashed out along my throat, over my collarbones, and settled right above one of the mounds of my heaving breasts.

"So sweet, *my female*," he growled.

I breathed out heavily and tried to absorb every single sensation moving through me, even if it seemed impossible. Never had I felt so exposed in the best of ways. Ren made me wet and so ready to take him into my body that I *ached*.

I felt like I was losing control, just like he was.

He pulled me closer to him, and I felt all of his hardness. He was so very masculine, so big and strong, and I felt tiny in comparison. Everything about him heightened my arousal.

"Mine," he growled as he sucked one of my nipples into his mouth, tugging at the peak with his teeth. A shiver worked its way through me, and I grabbed his head and tangled my fingers in his short, now disheveled dark strands.

He pulled back, his nostrils flaring as he inhaled deeply, his eyes now fully blue as he stared at me. With his mouth parted, I clearly saw the very sharp, very long twin canines that descended from his mouth and pricked at the bottom of his lip. I imagined what it would feel like to have those fangs embedded in my neck as he bit me and held me in place as he fully took me.

A shiver of pure lust shot through me, and I knew he smelled it, because he growled and gripped my waist right before flipping me over and positioning me on my hands and knees.

I moaned and thrust my ass back, this wanton side of me so unusual, but it felt so right. I felt how hard he was, his cock the biggest I could have ever imagined. And of course I thought about how in the hell he'd fit inside me. Even if I wasn't a virgin, that length and girth would be painful.

*And I've never anticipated anything more.*

And then he was kissing and licking all the way down my back; the growls that came from him had me rubbing my ass on his cock. I felt his fangs on my skin, and a shiver raced over me. His claws dug into my skin, not hard enough to break my flesh, but enough to let me know he wasn't fully human right now.

"*Mine*," he growled in that very animal-like, distorted voice, and I felt his warm breath along my ass. Another shiver violently raced up my spine.

He was rock-hard, so big and thick that wetness coated my inner thighs as my body prepared itself for his dick. Ren smoothed his hands over the cheeks of my ass, pawing them in his big hands before spreading them and groaning loudly.

"Perfection."

"*Ren*," I moaned his name now, lost and frenzied in my arousal. And when he had his mouth right between my thighs, licking and sucking at my primed pussy, I cried out and ground myself against his lips and tongue.

Yeah, I was *so* ready for Ren's claiming.

# TWENTY-FOUR

**Ren**

I was slowly losing control and had worried that my mate would be terrified of me. But here she was, so willing, wet, and ready for me, that I was damn near ready to come as it was.

*Mine.*

*Ours.*

I'd told her to run, because I knew the time had passed where I could try to be remotely human-like in my desire for her. But I also told her to flee, because I wanted so desperately to chase her, to hunt her down and take her.

"My female," I groaned at the sight of her on her hands and knees, her ass raised, her legs spread as far as they could go. She was pink and wet and smelled *incredible.* "I'll never get my fill of you. Never."

I attacked her core then, holding her perfectly shaped ass open as I ate out her pussy. Fuck, she was so sweet, her flavor an aphrodisiac. And all the while, she moaned and pushed her pussy back against my face, grinding herself on me as she sought her pleasure.

I reached down and palmed my cock, stroking myself furiously as I devoured her cunt. I was going to come, the first time of many tonight, and I planned on covering her flesh with my seed so she smelled like me and was marked every single way by me.

She moaned loud and long for more, and I plunged my tongue into her tight pussy, swallowing her honey and becoming instantly addicted to it. I'd never get enough.

"Ren, God, Ren, I'm going to... yes. *Yeeesss.*"

She came for me, her pussy getting wetter, that sweet nectar spilling from her. I greedily swallowed it, wanting more. I pumped my fist over my cock, harder and faster, the head slick with so much pre-cum the clear liquid dripped onto the forest floor.

My balls drew up tightly, and I roared against

her, the vibrations setting off another orgasm in her as she pressed her pussy even more against my mouth. I pulled back just in time, my orgasm rushing forward as I furiously jerked off, aiming the tip at her round ass and spread pussy. She was now braced on her elbows, her chest nearly touching the ground, her pussy in the air. I aimed right for that sweet spot. *Mine. Mine. Mine!*

I roared out and came hard, jet after jet of cum arcing out of the tip of my shaft and covering her pussy and ass in no doubt hotness. The white ropes had me roaring again, and all I wanted was to keep covering her with my seed so she smelled like me undeniably.

When the orgasm waned and I was panting, she lifted her upper body up so she was fully on her knees and stared back at me. Her eyes lowered to my cock and widened when she saw how hard I still was after coming.

"More, *mate*." I stood, taking hold of my shaft and giving the length another languid stroke.

She looked up at me, her long, dark hair fanned along her back, the desire clear on her face. I felt my balls draw up with another hardcore orgasm.

"Take me into your mouth, mate." She licked her lips, and I was riveted to the sight, imaging her mouth wrapped around my cock. "Tell me you're mine." My voice wasn't my own, rough and coarse, distorted from my animal.

"I'm yours," she said without hesitation.

"Yes," I growled. "You are mine. Only *mine*." I smoothed a finger along her bottom lip, my claw gently pushing along the supple flesh. She gasped, then moaned, and I felt another pulse of need shoot up the length of my cock. "Take me into your mouth. Suck on me." I kept moving my thumb back and forth along her bottom lip, slowly pulling it down, my heart thundering fiercely. "I am so hard for you, Mikalina. I ache to fill you with my seed." She made this soft noise, one that sounded like need and desperation, and everything that turned me on, everything that had the basic, primal male need to ease my mate's desire rising up in me.

I curled my hand behind her nape and pulled her closer. She gasped again, braced her hands on my thighs, and opened wide to suck the head in. I let my head fall back and moaned loudly, my voice echoing off the trees. Gods, it felt incredible. Never had I imagined it would be like this.

My cock throbbed, pulsed, and my balls were so damn tight I knew my second orgasm would be just as powerful as the first. Even now, I smelled my seed coating her skin from where I marked her, and that had my dick getting even harder for her.

She couldn't take all of me, not even half because I was so large, but she did it so fucking good I was on a razor's edge. Over and over, she sucked and licked at my shaft, moving her tongue around the tip to lap at my pre-cum, and the entire time, I gritted my teeth to hold off from coming. But when I couldn't stand it any longer, I gently pulled her back, gripped my length, and started stroking my cock furiously as I stared into her eyes. I gave a harsh roar of completion as I aimed at her supple, large breasts, covering the mounds with my seed, marking her on this part of her body as well.

And when the pleasure dimmed, I only had a moment of reprieve before the desire screamed in me once more.

*Take her.*

*Claim her.*

*Make her ours.*

I had her back on the ground, my hands under her, cushioning her, and started kissing her like a male who had lost all control. I pulled her close, needing her to all but crawl into me. Gods, I'd never get enough. I felt her breasts pressed to my chest, and another low growl left me, one I would never stop where my mate was concerned.

I kissed her neck, nipped her lightly, my canines aching to pierce her flesh. "I'll make it so you're marked by me, and all will know you are *mine*."

She made another small noise and dug her nails into my back, the sting and pain so fucking good.

I knew I had to claim her now.

I growled and dragged my hand up her belly and over her ribcage to cup one of her breasts. I thrust my hips forward, grinding my cock into her soft, wet, and hot pussy, closing my eyes and groaning in bliss.

*Fuck. Yes.*

I went back to sucking on her neck, dragging my tongue up the slender column, and thrusting back and forth into the cradle of her thighs, making her feel how hard and ready I was for her. I wanted to pierce her throat... ached to do just that. I wanted my scent in her bloodstream, wanted her to be fully mine. Pulling back was hard as hell, but I managed and breathed in deeply.

I forced myself to pull back to look down at her body, letting my gaze move up and down her slender form, memorizing every part of her. I finally stopped at her breasts once more, and although I already looked at them, touched them... sucked on them, I'd never get tired of gazing upon them.

*I'll never tire of her. I'll never be satiated. She's all I'll ever want.*

I was going to devour her.

I wrapped my hand around the nape of her neck, pulled her forward, and lowered my head so I could run my lips along her throat again, my Lycan needing to be at this particular part on her body, because I was salivating to mark her.

I was at the spot where her shoulder met her neck. I let her feel my canines, how long and sharp they were. It turned me on to hear her gasp from the sensation. Her flesh was sweet, addicting.

Everything about her was mine.

"Tell me what you're feeling."

She moaned. "So. Good. It all feels so good."

My cock grew harder at her admission.

While still lavishing attention on her throat, I reached down and tweaked her hard little nipples, the points stiff from her arousal and my ministrations. I was shaking with the force to keep calm, to stay under control.

"I've never done anything like this, Ren," she said, piercing through my fog of arousal. "I've never had a man touch me like this." Her voice was softer now. "I've never been with a man in any way."

I closed my eyes and groaned at the fact that my mate was untouched, completely pure. A virgin.

Like I was.

"You're the only woman I've ever wanted, Mikalina." I kissed at her pulse that beat wild and free at the base of her throat. "Even without knowing who you were, without seeing your face or scenting the intoxicating aroma that surrounds you, I saved myself only for you."

She moaned and leaned against me.

"My body is yours and has always been that way. Never will any other female feel me, see my wolf, feel my love. That is all for you. Only for you." I let go of her nipples and moved down to replace my fingers with my mouth. I sucked one of her turgid nipples into my mouth, her flesh sweet and silky soft. I alternated between peaks until she undiluted underneath me, begging softly for more.

My cock was so hard it ached. I ached. Right now, all I wanted to do was attack her like the fucking animal I was. I wanted to claim my mate hard and rough, as was the way of my kind.

"I don't want to hurt you, don't want to frighten you any more than I already have."

She thrashed her head back and forth, the scent of her arousal and of the wilderness surrounding me fueling my need for her and had my animal rising hard. "Be with me. Ease this ache in me, Ren."

And then she parted her thighs wider, and it was game fucking over.

I leaned away, my lips peeled back from my teeth, my fangs far too big at this point to even try to be concealed. The sight of her pussy lips spreading, showing me her pink, wet center, had me feeling like I was seconds from snapping and mounting her without even attempting to go slow.

*Take her. Claim her. Show her she's ours!*

I situated myself between her thighs, using my knees to spread her legs even wider for me. I moaned, about to come just from the sight of her so ready for me, from just the concentrated scent of her lust.

"Spread those pussy lips. Show me all that pink perfection."

And she obeyed me instantly, giving in to me in every single way I ever imagined.

All I could do was watch as my female reached down, spread her pussy lips wide, and showed me exactly what I owned.

# TWENTY-FIVE

**Mikalina**

I couldn't believe I was being so brazen, but it was like this fire burning in me, this other presence that told me I needed this... that *my mate* needed me to give myself over completely.

I touched myself, showing Ren the most intimate part of me. This made me feel so good knowing the sight of me exposed like this pleasured him.

*His pleasure is also mine.*

I let my gaze travel down his hard, muscular chest, one so broad and defined a little spasm of lust went through me. And then I stared at his huge cock. He was so... big, thick and long. All I could think about was how he wouldn't fit *all of that* inside me.

No way, yet I was greedy to try.

This man—werewolf—was brutal in his strength, and there was no doubt in my mind he could crush anyone who stood in his way. He stroked himself in slow, almost lazy motions, his focus on me... always on me. A drop of clear fluid, a little crystal of his need, was dotting the tip of his huge shaft, and I licked my lips. I remembered the flavor of him, dark spices and male power coating my tongue.

I finally lifted my gaze from his impressive length to his chest, over the light dusting of hair covering the golden flesh, up higher to the twin copper-colored nipples situated on his pecs, and finally stared at his face. I was more than ready to have him move even closer, to feel his big body right on top of mine, and feel him thrust deeply into me, claiming my virginity and giving me his.

Even now, I was still shocked to learn he saved himself for me. Only me.

His gaze trained between my splayed thighs as he said, "Keep them open for me, *mate*."

I wasn't about to disobey.

Ren stroked himself a little faster, the sound of his palm moving over his flesh filling my head, making me wetter. His bicep contracted and relaxed from the rapid motion of him jerking off.

"I need you," I moaned. "I ache for you, Ren."

He gave his shaft one more long stroke before grunting in almost pleasure/pain, and slamming his hands down on the ground on either side of my hips, his cock jutting forward and pressing against my soaked slit.

"I can never deny my female." He leaned down and kissed me soundly. "I'll give you more than you'll ever need, mate." The position he was in—and his words—made him look so very fierce.

He claimed my mouth harder and faster, forcing me to take all of him as he plunged his tongue between my lips, mimicking fucking me and what I wanted from him between my legs. His flavor was so spicy, dark, all male. I made a small noise in the back of my throat, unable to stop myself as need took over everything in me. And it was that small sound that seemed to have something snap inside Ren even more, just pushed his control right over the edge.

He moved his hand behind my head, grabbed a chunk of my hair, forcing my head back, my throat now arched. I felt the hot, hard length of him press hard between my thighs as he continued to kiss me and thrust against my legs at the same time. I wanted to feel him stretching me, pushing into my body and making the ache settle, making me feel full and complete.

"Yes, *Ren*."

As he stared into my eyes, his flashing blue with his animal right at the surface, he reached between us and placed the tip of his cock at the entrance of my pussy. Everything inside me stilled, tensed, and I panted with anticipation. The fierceness that covered his expression had my pulse skyrocketing.

"I'm taking what belongs to me, Mikalina."

I licked my lips, my pussy clenching, needing his length in me. "Yes. I'm yours." The words came so easily from me.

And as he started to slowly push into me, I knew he was trying to be gentle, to give my body time to adjust to his huge cock. I panted, sweat covering my body, my breath leaving me rapidly.

"So *tight*."

"Ahhh, you're too big."

"You were made for me," he gritted. "I was

made for you." And then he was all the way in me, and my back arched as I felt like I split in two. He claimed my virginity and gave me his. The pain was intense, the stretch burning, but he didn't move, allowing me to get used to the feel of him in my body.

His eyes were closed, his jaw clenched. His arms were locked tight on either side of my head, his biceps flexing from the strain not to move. The fullness was so shocking that I couldn't catch my breath.

"I'm sorry," he groaned. "Too good. Feels so tight. Been waiting for this my whole life." His words were broken up, his voice strained. When he started moving in and out of me, I dug my nails into his waist, holding on, giving myself up to him. I let my legs fall all the way open and accepted every hard inch of him.

He started speaking in his language again, and that just turned me on even more. The perspiration that covered his face and chest dripped onto me, arousing me further. His massive chest rose and fell as he breathed, and his big arms shook as he held himself up over me, clearly not completely letting go for my sake.

"I. Can't. Be. Gentle. Enough. My animal... *taking*

*over.*" He was more animal right now. I saw it on his face, felt it in his thrusting.

"Don't hold back." Maybe I shouldn't have said that, given this was my first time, but I wanted to experience Ren in all his hardened Lycan glory.

"*Fuck,*" he said harshly and seemed to lose control as he pushed into me and pulled out over and over, groaning with every thrust.

I felt my inner muscles clench rhythmically around his girth. The sensation was slightly uncomfortable because I was so sensitive, and because he filled me so completely.

"Watch as I claim you."

When the tip of his cock was lodged in the opening of my body once more, I rose up and braced my elbows on the ground to support myself, staring down as he slid that long, thick cock in and out of me. It disappeared before reappearing, slick and wet from my cream, streaks of virgin blood on the length.

"Watch as I fuck you, *mate.*"

He moved in and out of me, sweat dripping down his temples from his exertion and dripping onto my body. It singed my flesh, and I moaned for more. With each passing second, Ren picked up speed until he was slamming his dick into me back and forth. Over and over again.

"*Fuuuck*." His head was thrown back, his lips pulled back from his teeth as he groaned in pleasure. He looked so harsh and severe right now, and I grew even more turned on.

I couldn't hold myself up any longer and fell back onto the soft earth. He went even more primal on me then, the sound of our wet skin slapping together surrounding us and seeming to bounce off the trees in an erotic echo. It's all I could hear and *feel*.

*Yes. Yes. Yes.*

I thrashed my head back and forth, the pleasure building, my orgasm rushing up to explode within me.

"Come for me," he demanded harshly.

I cried out as I came for Ren, the pleasure so bright and hot and exquisite that I gasped for breath. And the whole entire time, he pounded into me, prolonging the pleasure, drawing more of that sweet torture from my spasming body.

"Sweet Jesus, baby. That's it."

Right before the tremors ended in me, Ren pulled out, which caused me to gasp at the sudden emptiness.

He had me flipped onto my hands and knees once more, spread my thighs as wide as they would go, then aligned the tip of his thick cock at my pussy. He only let me take one breath before he was shoving back into me, a roar leaving him and a gasp sounding from me.

He palmed my ass with his big hands, the act seeming very wolf-like. He gripped the mounds and squeezed them tightly until I moaned from the sensitivity of it.

"So fucking perfect." He slid his hands up to my waist and curled his fingers around me, pulling me back as he thrust forward, filling me over and over again.

"*Yes*," I found myself whispering. "More, Ren. God, more." I cried out the latter, and he growled. I knew he loved hearing me beg.

I let my head fall forward, looked down the length of my body, and could see the heavy weight of his balls swinging as he thrust in and out of me. I opened my mouth in a silent cry at how erotic the sight was.

He held onto my hips with a bruising force, so tight the pain had me gasping out, but also mixing with the pleasure, having me soar so high I'd never reach the ground again.

"Yes," he growled in that very Lycan voice of his.

I looked over my shoulder to stare into his face, seeing his animal flicker over his visage, his eyes glowing blue, his focus trained on me.

"Mine!" He buried himself deep inside me as he came, and it set off another mind-numbing orgasm in me. I could feel his cock jerk in my pussy, could feel the hard jets of his cum fill me.

With a deafening roar, Ren had his mouth at the side of my throat, where my neck and shoulder met, his canines piercing me and causing me to cry out.

And my pleasure went even higher as he held me down with his bite and still continued to fill me up with his orgasm.

Pulling his mouth away from my neck, he groaned out, "Mikalina. You're *mine*." He was over the edge in his control.

His breath came out in hard pants, bathing my flesh, a twin trail of blood starting to slip down my collarbone. He leaned forward again to lick at the wound, groaning anew.

My arms shook as I held myself up, the pleasure consuming me. And when he pulled out of me, I was about to collapse on the ground, but he moved quickly, now on his back with me pulled over him, my legs splayed on either side of his big body, the desire in me momentarily satiated.

Ren had one hand on the center of my back, the other between my thighs as if he needed to keep his semen in me. In fact, I heard him growl as he slid a finger deep into me, pushing in any cum that slipped out, causing me to shiver in need once more.

"My seed belongs in you, my female."

I moaned at his purely possessive words and tone. My skin was damp from sweat, my thighs sore from being spread wide, my pussy aching in the best way from losing my virginity to such a virile, potent male.

"Mmmm," he hummed in that male way of his. "*My female.* Nothing has ever felt so good as having you in my arms."

And then he just held me, the moonlight washing over us, the chill racing over my body having nothing to do with being cold and everything to do with the pleasure Ren had just given me.

"I can make you happy, mate. I can make you love me one day... as much as I love you."

I closed my eyes and smiled, knowing that I already loved this man. It was crazy and fast, but I'd never felt surer of anything else in my life.

I rose up and looked down at my big, strong

mate, and although it was a little strange saying that and a hell of a lot strange knowing it was now my reality, all I felt was contentment.

"I know you will. I already feel that way." His eyes flared with my admission, but I didn't let him say anything, just leaned down and was now the one to kiss him soundly.

# TWENTY-SIX

**Luca**

I left the manor when I sensed Ren come back with his female. There was no doubt he'd taken his mate in the way of our kind—under the light of the full moon, claiming her fully and placing his mark on her. It was the way of our species, a sacred, ritualistic act that mates did when they were finally complete with the woman meant to be theirs.

I wasn't strong enough to deny the pull of the moon, to let my Lycan fully out and run free; and every time the moon was high, I locked myself away, making my inner beast suffer with the pain of not being free one more time.

But on this night, I broke habit. Ren deserved to have this time in his home with his mate alone. He didn't need a brother who was slowly losing his mind bellowing in the very bottom chamber of the estate as he pulled his female close and reveled in the fact that he was no longer alone.

So here I was, walking the slightly worn path in the forest, the same one my brother clearly took night after night before he found his female. I could smell Ren's scent lingering within the trees, and the faint aroma of his claiming with the woman who was now irrevocably his for all time trailed in the wind.

I was happy for him, relieved we both wouldn't suffer the same fate.

And now here I was, taking the same path as he. But I'd long since lost the hope that he clearly hung onto all this time.

A break in the trees had the silvery glow from the moon casting down. I stepped into the clearing and tipped my head back, closing my eyes and letting that powerful pull almost lull me.

My brother would no doubt have the mating ceremony as soon as he could. He already claimed her—which I could easily smell in the air—but I knew he'd want our kind, as well as those in allegiance with the Lycans, to witness him mating his female properly. It was similar to a human wedding, but without the vows, the white dress, or the throwing of fucking rice. Basically, it was a way for our kind to show off our mates and to let the males know she was theirs—the mark on her neck on proud display. The word would travel between species so all knew not to fuck with her or they'd face death.

So yeah, my brother would most certainly be doing the ceremony as soon as possible. And I couldn't blame him. Hell, I would too.

I closed my eyes and exhaled, letting the glow from the moon try to soothe me as it always did. And it helped—minimally.

I knew rumors of me going mad had run rampant through our world. They all thought I was dangerous, violent, more beast than creature. I supposed I was. But for my brother, I'd make an appearance at his ceremony out of respect. I couldn't not go. And I'd look every one of those bastards in the eye and let them see I was still here —barely alive, but still here.

Then I'd crawl back into the pits of the manor and truly contemplate if it was all worth it anymore.

# TWENTY-SEVEN

**Ren**

I gave a mighty roar as I came, filling my mate up with my seed, making her take every single fucking ounce of it. She collapsed on top of me, her sweat dampening her little body that fit perfectly against mine. Our breathing was erratic, identical from just making love.

*No, I fucked my female good and hard. She'll be pleasantly sore tomorrow, remembering my cock deep in her body.*

I hummed at how good that made me feel.

For long moments, she just lay on top of me, my arms around her body, keeping her close. Needing her that way. I fucked her all night long, small intermissions of sleep and rest before I'd woken with a renewed insatiable hunger for her. I'd come so many times I was dizzy from my pleasure, exhausted from claiming my mate over and over again.

She was perfect in every way, unimaginably beautiful and all for me.

She rolled off me and lay on her back, her arms flung over her head, her eyes closed, and this small smile tilting her lips. I couldn't help myself from leaning over and kissing her long and slow, drugged-like. I could've gone again, my cock semi-hard but hardening once more as I looked down at her chest and saw her pert little nipples tighten further.

I blew a warm stream of air across them, and she arched and moaned even more.

I groaned and leaned forward, taking a peak into my mouth, sucking on it, licking the flesh, gently biting it. She arched and moaned, her legs sawing on the mattress.

I let go of her flesh with an audible pop and then pulled her in close, her chest to mine, her head resting on the crook of my arm. I had to stop touching her so erotically or I wouldn't have any control and I'd take her again and again.

And as much as I wanted to be with her once

more, I knew she had to be sore. She'd been so giving to me, spreading her thighs every time I needed her, welcoming me with her arms open as she held me and let me slide into her perfection until we both found release.

I loved this female, and although our bond as mates was unbreakable, I knew that even if we didn't have that fate-ordained connection, she was who I'd want in my life and by my side forever.

"I've never felt anything so good as having you in my arms," I murmured as exhaustion finally started to claim me. "Not in all my centuries in this world." I closed my eyes and smiled. "I'll never let you go." She moved closer to me, kissing my chest and sighing in contentment.

"Good, because I don't ever want you to let me go."

I growled at how fucking good that sounded from her lips. "Because I think I'm falling head over heels, madly in love with you, Ren."

My body went tight, my heart racing. And then I closed my eyes as pure pleasure washed through me.

"I know it's insane, seeing as things have moved so fast. But I can't deny that I've never felt this way about anyone, never even dreamed of it." She tipped her head back to look into my face. "And what else can it be besides love?" Her voice was so soft.

I cupped the side of her face, stroking a finger over her cheek. "You make my heart ache, my blood rush, and every protective instinct in me come alive. Even if I'd only ever gotten this one moment in time with you, every lonely second of my existence would have been worth it." I leaned in and kissed her. "I love you, my female. More than you'll ever know, more than you can ever comprehend." I kissed her once more, sealing those words between us. She rested her head on my bicep once again, and we stayed silent for so long I wondered if she'd fallen asleep.

But then she whispered, "Will you show me your animal?" Her voice was soft, her tone inquiring.

My Lycan rose up, anxious, excited to show our mate what he looked like. I pushed him back, fearful of what Mikalina would think about him. He wasn't a normal-appearing wolf. My beast was massive, corded with power and muscular, and stuff terrifying legends were made of.

"I don't want to frighten you." Although I desperately wanted her to see my inner animal, it was a fearsome fucking creature. She wasn't fully used to this new supernatural world, and I worried about shocking her.

"Will your animal hurt m—"

"Never," I said with so much firmness there was no doubt about that lone word. "He only wants to please and protect you. He wants to always provide for you. We are one in the same, and everything I feel for you in my human side is magnified by my animal side tenfold."

She was silent for long seconds, just letting me hold her and rub my hand up and down her bare, warm back.

"I trust you with my life," she said softly and tipped her head back to look into my face. "I've never trusted anyone more, Ren. I want to see him."

And the sound of her saying she wanted to see my wolf had the beast rising up excitedly again, feeling pleasure that our mate wanted to see him fully.

I couldn't deny her anything, even if it worried me that I'd terrify my mate with the sight of the feral creature I housed within me.

I leaned in and kissed her slowly before murmuring, "Okay. He's yours the same as I am. Forever."

# TWENTY-EIGHT

### Ren

After we'd gotten dressed and ate a light breakfast of fruit and juice, homemade bread, pastries, and jam, I felt my female sigh contentedly in my arms. She was happy, because of me, and damn if that didn't please me to no end.

It was as if she couldn't be parted from me, and because I was more animal than man and was possessive of her and her time, this also fucking pleased me immensely.

The servants had been moving around the castle with purpose, and I could see she wasn't used to having people wait on her, but the more she saw them and how much they enjoyed their job, how well I treated them because I saw them as an extension of my family, the more I felt her get used to the idea.

I led her out of the manor and toward the house, wanting privacy for what I was about to show her. And I couldn't help but look at her constantly, smiling at how fucking lucky I was. I found myself continuously thanking whoever listened that I'd been granted my mate after waiting for so long.

But even my happiness for her couldn't dim how tense I was. My body was tight, because a part of me dreaded this. I worried about what she'd think about me after I showed her my wolf.

"I care for you, Ren. So much." We stopped, and she rose on her toes to place her palms on my shoulders, smiling up at me. "Your inner animal is an extension of you, so your fear isn't needed, because I'll love him as much as I love you," she said as if she read my mind.

I leaned down and kissed her for long seconds, continued to kiss her until she was breathless and I had to force myself to take a step back or I'd take her right up against a tree.

We walked for another ten minutes, my hand wrapped around her, keeping her close. Finally, I stopped, exhaling, feeling my wolf pacing in me, desperate to get this going and show our mate what he was. He wanted her to see how big he was, to know that he could protect her no matter what.

I stared at Mikalina, gathering my courage to do this. Although this was the most natural thing for me, to show her this side of me, frightening her when I just found her went against everything in me.

But our connection was undeniable. Unbreakable. Irrevocable. And as the years passed, it would grow. And I wanted my female to see me in all ways, to know what she was truly getting herself into by mating me.

I'd taken her to a secluded place in the woods on my property. Did she know all of this was hers, *ours*? For as far as the eye could see, from the edge of one town to the border of another, it was ours.

And today, I'd show a female—*my female*—my Lycan for the very first time.

I pulled her in close, kissing the top of her head and closing my eyes, just inhaling the sweet scent that filtered around her. She tightened her arms around me.

"I'm ready," she whispered against my chest, and I nodded, even though she couldn't see me.

I leaned down and kissed her once more before taking a step back and going for my shirt. I kept my eyes on hers as I started unbuttoning it before shrugging it off my shoulders. Then I stood there for a second, letting her gaze roam over my chest, smelling her heightened arousal coating the air. I couldn't stop my body from reacting. My cock thickened, and a growl erupted from me.

Then I turned, showing her my back, hearing her gasp. I looked over my shoulder to gauge her reaction. She was staring wide-eyed at the wolf tattoo that covered the entire expanse from shoulder to waist.

"This is my Lycan." During the claiming, I hadn't been in a position to allow her to actually see my back, so frenzied and wild in the mating. But now, I let her look her fill.

She stepped closer and reached out, but before she touched my flesh, she curled her fingers toward her palm.

"No, love. Touch me. Touch *him*."

She traced the outer edge of the marking, and my Lycan rubbed against her touch, whether she realized it or not.

"It's incredible," she said with awe in her voice. "The artistry is amazing. So lifelike."

I slowly shook my head and turned to face her, taking her hands in mine and bringing them to my lips to kiss her knuckles. "It's a part of me. I was born with it, as is every male Lycan. That is, in essence, our inner animal, always with us even when it can't be seen by the naked eye." I gave her hands one more kiss before stepping back and going for my pants. I saw her eyes glaze over with arousal once I had them off, and couldn't help but smirk. My female was insatiable.

And then I closed my eyes and let my human side fall back, let my wolf come forward.

The change happened far too fast for me to feel anything but immense power claiming me. But I was aware of my skin changing to fur, my bones breaking and realigning, and my nails turning to claws. The shift didn't bring me anything but pure, unadulterated freedom as I gave into everything that I was and let my other half rise up.

When I opened my eyes again, it was to see my female staring at me with shock on her face. I scented the air but smelled no fear, only astonishment and wonder. Her heart was racing, a *thunk-thunk, thunk-thunk* rhythm that had me tentatively taking a step forward. Although my Lycan was now the one in control, my human side was still very much present to rationalize and observe. I was always with her, no matter what.

In my wolf form, I was triple my weight, the size of a horse standing tall. I was the most powerful creature on the planet, strong and unstoppable, and with my mate, nothing and no one would ever defeat me, because I'd always have the fire burning in me to protect her at all costs.

*Come to me.*

She couldn't hear me, wouldn't understand the noises my wolf made in pleasure because of her very presence, but she did walk forward, her breathing erratic, this no doubt another shock to her system.

My beast took a step forward, his massive body dwarfing her.

"God," she breathed out as she tilted her head back to gaze at me. "You're so big."

My wolf dropped down to his hind legs so we were more eye level, so she didn't feel so intimidated by his size.

Her pulse was beating so hard at the base of her throat, and she licked her lips and reached her hand out.

*You own every part of us, our female.*

"This is all so... unreal."

My beast made a sound deep in his throat, a soft

growl to encourage her to touch me. And then she touched the creature, and he closed his eyes, snuffling out a deep breath as if he'd been holding it in.

*Yes, that's right. She* is *really here with us. She is really ours.*

She explored the wolf for long moments, touching his ears, his paws, running her fingers over his snout, along his jaw. If he could have purred like a feline, I knew he would have for how good her touch felt.

He'd been waiting for this for over three hundred years too.

Feeling her acceptance of me and my animal was a shock to *my* senses, one I'd never take for granted.

"I love you... all of you. Every single strange and magical part of you, Ren." She smiled and shocked the fuck out of me by kissing the tip of the great beast's nose. And the bastard melted for her right then and there all over again.

He was putty in her hands, a potentially violent, aggressive killing machine that would only ever submit its dominance to this one female.

"I've never seen anything as beautiful," she murmured to my beast, and in return, he growled low, the pleasure not one of aggression but immense love. "So big and strong. I bet you won't let anyone or anything ever hurt me, isn't that right?"

The beast butted his head up against her hand, and she made a soft sound.

My Lycan rubbed its massive head against her, wanting his scent all over her. And she let him. She closed her eyes and sighed, wrapping her arms around his neck. Although he'd never let anything take that kind of dominant stand, with her, we were putty at her feet, willing to do anything she wanted as long as she looked at us with love in her eyes.

He was as possessive of her as I was.

We stayed that way for long moments, her holding my animal, the beast becoming calm and comforted, at ease in her presence for the first time in its life.

We both knew one thing for certain, my wolf and me.

*She was ours.*

# TWENTY-NINE

**Mikalina**

*Several weeks later*

I stared at myself, and the woman in the reflection looked scared shitless.

Wide eyes. Pale flesh. Ruby-red lips. A trembling body.

A mating ceremony. A sacred ritual when a Lycan found his mate. This was important to Ren—to his kind—and even if I was scared of the unknown, I was excited about the prospect of starting this new life.

The dress I wore was this light-blue color, sheer and ultra-feminine. The bodice was lacy, accenting my breasts, and screamed innocence. The material flowed down my legs from the bodice, pooling at the ground. My feet were bare, apparently what the female was supposed to do, as Lycan's were of the earth, their beasts of Mother Nature.

I ran my fingers along the beading detail that was sporadically placed along the skirting. It was the most gorgeous dress I'd ever seen, something I would have picked out for myself. But what shocked me the most was that Ren had this gown made specially for his mate—for me—centuries before.

Even thinking that, knowing he'd been anticipating meeting me his entire life, had me falling more in love with my big wolf-shifting mate. I had a feeling it would always be a little surreal.

I smoothed my hands over the soft, silky material once more and stared at the mark on my neck. It had since healed, but the scar would forever faintly cover my throat, and I felt a thrill at that. To think this mark would have my aging stall, allowing me to spend year after year, century after century, with Ren was... fantastical.

My heart skipped in my chest at that thought.

I sensed him before he even said a word and lifted my head to look over my shoulder, seeing my big, strong Lycan standing in the doorway. Ren took up the entire space, his shoulders so wide, his chest so broad. He looked so damn good as he watched me with barely restrained heat in his eyes.

He wore a crisp white shirt, the first few buttons undone at the collar to show off his masculine, tan throat. His gray slacks weren't flashy, but I knew they were made just for him, uniquely tailored, and expensive as hell.

I wasn't quite sure what to expect tonight, just knew this was something very special and sacred to Ren's kind. And since this was my world now, I was more than happy to participate in anything he wanted. I wanted to fully immerse myself in this life.

"Come here, my female." His voice was a low rumble, and I shivered in response, walking up to him without any hesitation at all.

He held his arms out to me, and I went into them so very willingly, sinking against the hard planes of his chest, my head barely reaching his pectoral muscles. And he just held me, whispering words in his native language, ones that I knew were endearments, sweet things about starting our life together, about loving me.

He told me the mating ceremony went far beyond human marriage. Even if we hadn't done an actual ceremony, there was no breaking the bond we had, the mark he'd given me. We were forever linked. And I believed that—felt it—with all my heart.

Just looking at him now made a flush rise up right underneath my skin. My body became hyper-aware, the blood rushing through my veins. And my heart picked up speed.

I tipped my head back and smiled at him, and he lifted a hand to cup the side of my face, smoothing his thumb along my cheek, his eyes flashing blue as his animal rose up.

"I love you," I whispered, and he closed his eyes and groaned as if those three words were the very best thing he'd ever heard.

"And I love you. So much you make me ache in the best of ways."

Now it was my turn to smile as a giddiness filled me.

"Are you ready for this? Are you ready for forever?"

I opened my eyes, feeling soft and warm, protected against him. "I don't think I've ever been more ready for anything in my life."

And I hadn't been. He was my future... the one I'd been patiently waiting for.

# THIRTY

**Ainslee**

I felt out of place, but then again, I guess in a way I was in a whole other world. Romania, especially in these little villages, was so unlike the Highlands I called home. But this country was definitely beautiful nonetheless.

*I've always felt out of place, have I not?*

I moved around the room, keeping to the walls, because I felt slightly claustrophobic. I saw my father and mother. The love they had for each other was so very real.

My father, King of the Scottish Lycan Clan, had found his mate in my mother, an American vampire who'd been living in Eastern Europe since she turned eighteen over a century before. Their meeting had been nothing short of happenstance, luck of the draw, a strike of fate, or one of the many other sayings my father liked to use to describe them meeting.

It was a story I loved hearing more than once while growing up as I curled up on the massive leather couch that was in front of the roaring fire in our hunting lodge mansion. I listened to my father tell the story as he stared at his mate, the love, longing, and gratitude that he had her in his life clear on his face.

To say opposites attracted was an understatement where my parents were concerned.

It was something every supernatural—and mortal human—strived for, wasn't it? To have... love?

I glanced over at my brothers, seeing them tossing back drinks like it was water and they'd been in the desert for far too long. They were so much like my father—taking after their Lycan sides with gusto. Those wolf sides dominated their vampire halves, so all that was left were feral beasts.

But me? Neither of my sides had claimed dominance. I was neither full vampire nor Lycan. A true mix of both, a little bit from one side, a dash from the other. I was barely stronger than a mere human, because apparently my body didn't want to decide which genetic side to let dominate in utero.

I exhaled, once again frustrated with myself because I cared about any of that, when in the grand scheme of things, I should just be happy I had a loving family and centuries to look forward to.

*But I do care. I care, because every male in my family looks at me as if I'll break.* I'm coddled and protected. Hell, I'm surprised I was able to come to the mating ceremony at all, seeing as they think I'm some delicate freaking flower.

Once again, I scanned the room. Vampires, Lycans, demons, and even a few other creatures from the supernatural world had traveled far and wide to witness the mating ceremony. All of these creatures were either friends or allies with Ren and or the Lycans. And it was surreal to see. Because the males in my family were so protective, the only creatures of my world I'd seen were the wolves and vampires.

So this was exciting as much as it was a little terrifying.

My mother gestured me over and gave me a smile, her twin tiny fangs coming into view for a second before she curled her arm around my shoulders and pulled me in close. Her long black hair was pulled into a stylish chignon, her deep sapphire-colored gown complementing her pale flesh and light-blue eyes.

"Ah, there's my wee lass. Come here, darling daughter." My father, a massive Lycan with broad shoulders and a mammoth frame, towered over many of the guests at the mating ceremony. But then again, not many creatures were as big and fearsome as a Lycan, or a king for that matter. And my father was both.

I smiled up at him, and he leaned down to kiss me on top of the head. Never mind that I was twenty years old—an adult in human standards—because in Lycan standards, my father still saw me as his little girl, so very young when you looked at the lifespan of a paranormal creature.

"Yer mother and I will be leaving this time tomorrow night."

My father had bought a private jet for my mother for obvious reasons: sunlight was a no-go for vampires, as was commercial airlines being far too dangerous. Then there was also the fact that he just liked to dote on her, giving her presents, buying her things because he liked to see the smile on her face, but he also loved—probably more so—the goodhearted annoyance of her telling him to quit buying her things.

"Mayhap we'll stop up north on the way home, let ye see the Northern Lights?" He grinned broadly, knowing I loved seeing those beautiful lights, and even though I could tolerate some sunlight, I preferred to keep the same hours as my mother and father—which was being pretty much nocturnal.

"They'll bitch," I grumbled as I tipped my chin in the direction of my three brothers. The triplets were as rowdy as you'd come to expect Lycan males to be, but then again, they fit right in with the clan. I was more the oddball out.

"Ach, those little shites are all too ready tae make their baby sister happy."

I shook my head but smiled. Yeah, they were the best, even if I gave them a hard time for being so damn overbearing and protective.

My father started speaking with another clan member, and I scanned the room. Crystal glasses with blood were filled for the vampires. Dark-colored whiskey or bourbon for the other guests. There was a massive banquet table with every kind of food imaginable.

I reached out and grabbed a glass of champagne from a passing waiter, smiled, and said thank you, then brought the glass to my mouth to take a sip of the sweet, bubbly liquid. Although it wasn't as sweet as blood and didn't give me the euphoric high the life-giving liquid did, it would still do the job well enough.

I finished nearly the whole glass—feeling the effects of the alcohol move through me pleasurably —when I felt this shift in the massive hall. The air seemed to get colder, and as if in unison, everyone turned and faced the wide entrance of the great hall.

They were looking at someone.

I was small, not just for a female, but also for a supernatural creature, so there was no way I could see over the towering males or the svelte, tall females.

I inhaled deeply, sifting through all the scents in the room and trying to focus on whatever was at that entrance. It took work; the scents were many and thick, perfumes and foods, but then I locked on it.

I felt this jolt move through me at the scent. And once it filled my nose and head, I could smell nothing else.

A Lycan male was who everyone was looking at, yet I still couldn't see him. I shivered, not under-standing why I suddenly felt so hot and cold.

"Is that Luca Lupineov?" my mother whispered to my father, sidling closer to him. He wrapped one arm around my mother's waist, and as if he wanted to keep the females close, he did the same to me, bringing me protectively to his side.

I noticed my brothers pushed their way toward us, their looks dark, dangerous. They scanned their eyes over my mother and me, protective of us just as our father was. Then again, this was how all supernatural males were when it concerned females they cared about.

I glanced around the room, taking note males did the same with their mates and daughters, brothers seeming to instinctively want to protect their sisters and mothers.

"Aye," my father answered, and I felt his hand tighten on my shoulder. "A Lycan gone mad is one of the most dangerous creatures alive."

And then bodies started to part as the male was clearly moving into the great hall. I still couldn't see him and tried to rise on my toes to get a better look. I saw a flash of dark, short hair, a set of wide, powerful shoulders. The male straightened, and I gasped at how big and tall he was, towering over even my father, who by all accounts was one of the biggest males in this room.

Lord, that male had to be easily six-foot eight. And the power in his body, the stacks of muscles, was staggering. But there was something else, something about him that had my skin tightening and this strange feeling moving within me. I felt my father stiffen and glanced up at him. He was looking at me with his brows drawn.

"Lass, are ye okay?"

I cleared my throat and tried to calm my heart— which of course only made things worse. "I'm fine." I hoped my smile was convincing. But my father still watched me for long seconds until movement up ahead drew his attention.

I exhaled and heard low murmurs.

It was *his*... the Lycan male's, Luca's voice.

I actually closed my eyes and would have swayed from the sound if not for the fact that my father held onto me.

Luca was congratulating his brother Ren on his mating, and his deep, husky, and accented voice did warm things to me.

But why?

I'd heard about Luca Lupineov, the Lycan shifter who'd slowly lost his mind because he hadn't found his mate. I knew it happened on occasion, centuries passing for our kind in the paranormal world making life tedious and hope fading.

*More beast than male*, I heard him being called. Hell, the rumors of Luca had reached all the way to the Highlands.

The murmurs in the room were low but great, and I sensed he was leaving. The bodies parted once again, and there I finally saw him, his back to me, twenty feet separating us and growing more as he exited.

And yeah, he was even more massive and imposing than any other male in this room.

*He really is more animal than male.*

"*Luca,*" I said his name so low I knew only I'd have heard. I didn't even know why I said his name, to be honest. It just slipped from my lips as if it were a plea.

But then he stilled. His huge body freezing, his hands curling into themselves as he snapped his head up. I swore I heard him inhale, felt my eyes widen as the room seemed to grow even colder. Everyone was at a standstill at whatever was happening. Would he lose control and kill someone? Was his mind so deteriorated that we were all in danger?

My father was in the process of pulling my

mother and me behind him, my brothers coming forward to make a wall, blocking us from Luca. But the big Lycan spun around, his glowing animal-like blue eyes swinging back and forth as he scanned the hall. And then our eyes locked, gazes clashing.

"*You*," he growled, his lips peeling back from his teeth, his canines growing as he stared right in my eyes. "*My mate*," he all but purred, but it sounded so very wolf-like.

I sensed every male in the room going to protect the females. My brothers were making a barricade around me, but I kept trying to see through the openings their big bodies made, as if I couldn't drag my gaze from the huge Lycan. God, he really was more animal than man, his body seeming to grow even bigger as his beast pushed forward.

My brothers' bodies seemed to grow as well.

"Oh, feck no," Caelan ground out.

"No fecking way some crazy-ass Lycan is getting tae her," Tavish seethed.

"I've been itching for a fight, and what better one than tae go toe-tae-toe with that crazy mother-fecker?" I could hear the glee in Lenox's voice.

"Watch yerselves, sons," my father growled. "Our priority is getting yer mother and yer sister out."

I glanced over my shoulder and looked into my father's face. He was staring at me, his eyes flashing blue from his wolf.

"Because that Lycan won't stop until he gets tae his prize."

*Me.*

Yeah, my father meant me.

I started shaking.

"Tis okay, lass. We will no' let him get tae ye."

I didn't want to tell my father I didn't shiver from fear but from... anticipation.

I snapped my focus back to Luca. He still looked at me, and I knew he hadn't taken his gaze off me at all. His grin widened. God, his incisors were so big and white... so long and sharp.

As he watched my father and brothers take a protective stance, he chuckled low, deep, the sound distorted because of his beast. That laugh told me one thing—nothing would keep him from getting to me, not even four full-grown Lycans, or hell, a roomful of dangerous males.

Luca lifted his hand, his finger pointing to me. "*Female.*" My heart was thundering in my chest. "*You. Are. Mine.*"

And that's when all hell broke loose.

# THIRTY-ONE

**Mikalina**

*A week later*

It had been seven days since I'd gone through the mating ceremony with Ren, and although it felt like I'd known this male my entire life—the connection that strong—I was also experiencing this new life with him and reveling in it all.

I thought about the phone call I'd made to my parents, telling them I planned on staying in Romania indefinitely. What was the biggest hit was the fact that they didn't seem the least bit upset about it, that they didn't even ask when they'd see me again. Was I so forgettable to them?

I lay in the massive bed we shared and stared at

the hearth, pushing away those feelings, because in the end, it didn't matter. What did matter was knowing that the man beside me was mine forever and that there would never be a hole in my heart as long as I had him.

I thought about my new home, and a smile formed on my lips. The castle was massive, and although it had been modernized, there were still the aesthetics of it being old world. The fireplace wasn't necessarily needed, but it was lovely, especially during these chilly nights.

I thought back to just last week and how things had gone great... until shit hit the fan, so to speak. My mating ceremony, although making me feel like I was thrust into another world, had been perfect and felt so right. And when Luca actually made an appearance, congratulating Ren and me on our mating, I knew that meant the world to my mate.

It meant the world to me, because I knew how much Ren needed to see his brother, and because I knew it was probably so hard for Luca to be around everyone. Especially during our mating, since he was still without his female.

I was learning so much about this strange new world. It was confusing at times, frightening and awe-inspiring, but I had Ren at my side and knew that as long as he was in my life, I could get through anything. Even if it seemed like a massive fairy tale.

I rolled over and curled up against my big, strong, Lycan male. He slept soundly beside me, his sometimes harsh and masculine face now at rest. His dark eyelashes were crescents along his cheeks, and I found myself smiling. He curled his hand around my waist, still asleep, but always having to be touching me, as if he couldn't stop himself from keeping me close.

He slowly opened his eyes, the irises flaring light-blue from his Lycan being pleased at seeing me before slowly changing to that warm whiskey color I loved so much.

To know my life had always been leading me here was still a shock. I remembered Mini's words that first night of my arrival to Dobravina, how it was said long ago about my arrival. I may not know every little detail about folktales, prophecies, or the like, but what I did know was that everything I'd ever gone through in life had led me to the moment where I met Ren.

"*My female*," he growled in pleasure, and I couldn't stop from smiling at how that deep, serrated sound always had me instantly ready for him. But reality and my thoughts were a bucket of cold water on my growing desire.

"What's wrong?" Ren asked in all seriousness, my protective mate hating to see me distressed. Heck, I stubbed my toe last night walking up the stone steps, and the way he acted you would have thought I'd gotten a limb torn off.

"Do you think Luca will be okay? Do you think they'll let him have her?" I didn't know why I thought to talk about this right now. We'd spoken of this a few times during the last week, but it wasn't like Ren knew any better than me—or hell, even Luca for that matter—on how things would play out.

Ren exhaled and pulled me in closer, tucking me against him and just holding me. "She's his mate, and he has every right to her, but she's also the daughter of the Scottish Lycan King, and the younger sister to very protective older brothers. That in itself will be complicated. His biggest road-block. Or maybe it'll be that she won't want him.

I felt my eyes widen. "A mate... may not want the other? I don't understand. I thought it was all... like, for sure." I sounded so very ignorant, but Ren just kissed me on the top of my head and pulled me in even closer.

"She no doubt feels the connection and pull toward him. And I have no doubt she wants him, but she's very young, from what I know of her, and her family coddles her. She's probably not experienced any of the outside world much, and if she has, it's been under the watchful eye of those overbearing males in her family." He exhaled slowly. "But I can't say her family doesn't have reason to be weary of my brother."

I leaned back slightly to look in his face. "I don't understand. Aren't you happy about this, about Luca finding his mate after all this time?"

"Because my brother hasn't been right here—" He tapped his head. "—for a long time, my female." He smoothed a hand over my hair, then leaned down to kiss my forehead. "So I understand their wariness. If I had a daughter, I'd probably keep her away from a Lycan who'd gone mad too." He smiled slowly at me. "But my brother is resilient. He's held on this long, and there's no way he's giving up that female. They have a fight on their hands with Luca. Gods save them." He chuckled, and his lighthearted attitude gave me hope that things would work out.

I may not know Luca all that well, only met him for that brief time at our mating ceremony, but my heart broke for him, and he was family now. My family. How strange—again—I felt more of a connection with a virtual stranger than I did with my own parents.

"No more thinking about this, Mikalina. No more worrying about what we have no control over."

I didn't like thinking like that, but I knew Ren was right. I had no control over this. It was fate, destiny, whatever you wanted to call it. But I was glad Luca found his mate, even if he had a fight on his hands with her and her family.

The longer I was pressed against Ren, the more my stress faded and my body heated.

"Mmmm," Ren growled, no doubt sensing my arousal. "Is my mate hungry?" He rolled his hips, and I moaned at the feel of his massive erection rubbing along my belly, the tip slick with pre-cum. And then I made a surprised noise as he pulled me on top of him.

My legs were on either side of his muscular thighs, and a gasp of pleasure left me to feel that stiff length pressed right to my bare sex.

"I'm always—" I ground myself against him, already pleasantly naked from the last round of making love we'd done just earlier in the evening, "—hungry—", my mating mark on the side of my throat warmed, hummed. Arousal and heat swirled within me, "—for you." I moaned again. "And only —" I rose up, placed the thick tip of his cock at my entrance, and sank down, crying out, "—for you, Ren." *Only ever for you.*

And then he fucked me for the rest of the night... exactly how I wanted him to.

# EPILOGUE

**Ren**

*Two years later*

I knew she was miserable, her body aching, her new shape something she was getting used to daily. But gods, I loved seeing Mikalina big with my children.

Twin boys. Sons.

I was blessed many times over.

I could smell how strong the Lycan genes were in them, little wolves I'd teach how to hunt, how to control the power they'd wield as they grew.

And I wanted Mikalina to teach them about humans, about her side, her customs, and what she

I wanted them to know both sides of where they came from.

"Andrei told me Mini made the babies some blankets. They'd like to bring them over in a couple of days." I glanced toward the opening of the bathroom, where Mikalina was getting ready for bed. "I bet they are gorgeous. Andrei said she's been working on them for months."

I had no doubt they would be beautiful, and I loved that my mate was happy. Because her happiness was mine.

"I don't think I can get much bigger," she idly said as she came out of the bathroom, rubbing lotion on her beautiful big and round belly. "Yeah, I'm pretty sure I'm at capacity, yet I have another eight weeks to go." She glanced up at me, her brows pulled low. "You sure Lycan's don't go before the whole human nine-month mark?"

I chuckled and leaned back fully against the wooden headboard, clasping my hands behind my head and just staring at her.

"I think you look gorgeous. And sexy," I growled the latter out, and she cocked an eyebrow at me before adjusting my shirt, which hung off of her even pregnant.

"You are insatiable."

I beckoned her closer and grinned when she came. "I sure am. With you. Only you." I gently pulled her onto the bed, then adjusted her so she was curled against my side, my arm around her shoulders, the feeling of being content because my mate was in my arms washing through me.

"Are you up for watching a movie tonight?"

"I'm game for anything you want to do."

She tipped her head back and wagged her brows. "Anything?" Her voice was low and sultry, and I felt heat coil in my gut.

My cock punched forward hard and incessant, the need to be buried in her tight pussy claiming me. "Anything," I growled.

She sat up, pushed the long fall of her hair off her shoulder, and turned around so her legs were outstretched and her feet by my hands. At first, I wasn't sure what she was doing, not until she wiggled her toes, wagged her brows, and pulled a chuckle from me.

I lifted her tiny foot and started gently massaging and kneading the heel, then moved to the toes. She rested back on her hands and closed her eyes, moaning softly. "That's it. Right there."

I grinned, her voice so sexual, even if it was just from the foot massage.

"I need this nightly, please and thanks."

I laughed louder, deeper, and she opened her eyes and grinned. "I already massage you nightly, my female."

She tipped her head to the side. "I mean, yeah, but maybe I can get you to do it twice a day?" She pouted playfully.

I'd give her anything. Anything. My sole purpose in this life was pleasing her and providing for my mate. "This isn't a hardship, sweetness, and something I'm eager to provide for you. It kind of turns me on."

She lifted a brow. "Rubbing my feet turns you on? Didn't realize you were into that kind of kink."

I purred. "When it comes to you, I'm into everything." And just like that, the playfulness was gone. Her eyes went half-lidded, and the scent of her pussy becoming wet from her arousal slammed into my nose.

"Then hurry up with the foot massage, my big, bad wolf, because I'm feeling like we need to skip to the bonus feature."

She didn't have to say it twice.

**The End**

Want to read more in The Lycans series? Check out
**You Are Mine,** Luca and Ainslee's story, out now!

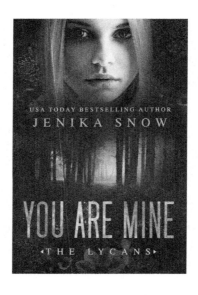

# About the Author

*Find Jenika at:*

www.JenikaSnow.com

Jenika_Snow@yahoo.com

Printed in Great Britain
by Amazon

79325080R00129